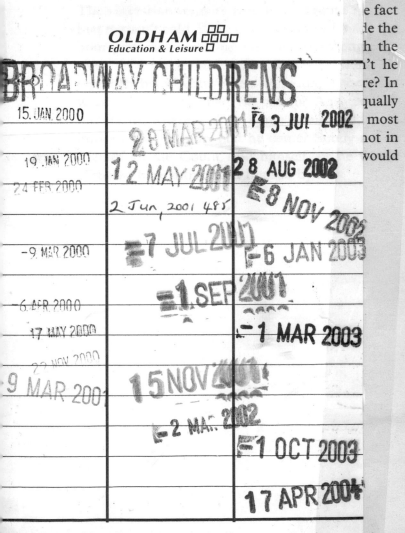

e fact
...de the
...h the
...'t he
...re? In
...qually
...most
...not in
...would

BITE INTO THE VAMPIRE SERIES –
IT'S FANGTASTIC!

VAMPIRE ISLAND

Willis Hall

ILLUSTRATED BY
TONY ROSS

RED FOX

A Red Fox Book

Published by Random House Children's Books
20 Vauxhall Bridge Road, London, SW1V 2SA

A division of The Random House Group Ltd
London Melbourne Sydney Auckland
Johannesburg and agencies throughout the world

First published by Red Fox 1999

Printed and bound in Great Britain by
Cox & Wyman Limited, Reading, Berkshire

Papers used by The Random House Group Limited
are natural, recyclable products made from wood grown in
sustainable forests. The manufacturing processes conform to
the environmental regulations of the country of origin.

THE RANDOM HOUSE GROUP Limited Reg. No. 954009

ISBN 0 090 965351 6

1

"Swish-THUNK!" . . . *"Swish-THUNK!"*

There was a full moon hanging low over the tree tops, and the only sounds that could be heard came from the pit, two metres in depth, as the two shovels struck at the soft earth at the bottom of the hole, then tossed it up and out on to the Transylvanian forest clearing.

"Swish-THUNK!" . . . *"Swish-THUNK!"*

"How much deeper do we need to go, Emil?" asked one of the diggers, nervously. He was a tall, thin man with a drooping moustache and anxious eyes. His name was Ernst Tigelwurst. He drove a bullock-cart for his living and he was unused to being in the forest so late at night.

"Deeper than we've gone already," growled Emil Gruff, a short, thick-set, red-bearded, short tempered man who, by day, worked as a woodcutter in that same forest. "Stop chattering, Ernst, and get on with the job in hand."

"Swish-THUNK!" . . . *"Swish-THUNK!"*

"How much did you say this foreigner will pay us, if the plan succeeds?" asked Tigelwurst. "And will we get the money in good, honest grobeks, or will it be in foreign currency?"

"You will get more than the job is worth, be sure of that," snarled the woodcutter. "Stop worrying about how much you'll have in your pocket, or in which coinage it will come – first, earn it!"

"Swish-THUNK!" . . . *"Swish-THUNK!"* . . . *"Swish-THUNK!"* . . . *"Swish-THUNK!"*

Stung by the woodcutter's sharp reprimand, Ernst Tigelwurst held his tongue and stuck to his task. The pit grew steadily deeper as both men shovelled away in silence. A long dark cloud drifted across the face of the moon, casting shadows across the little forest clearing. The only light to guide them as they worked came from a flickering lantern that Emil Gruff had brought along and which stood at ground level on the rim of the pit, bathing the earth walls and floor in an eerie orange glow.

"Ter-WHOOOooo!"

Ernst Tigelwurst recognised the owl's cry, coming from somewhere off in the dark of the trees, and he shivered as he felt the hairs rise along the back of his neck. It was not fear of the bird of prey that had caused the carter's anxiety – but its presence had reminded him that there were other and more terrible creatures dwelling in the forest.

There were, of course, the wolves of Tolokovin. A fearsome pack of sharp-toothed, cunning beasts that roamed the wide-ranging forest by day, causing the simple peasants of Tolokovin to murmur the name of their patron saint, Unfortunato, and then cross themselves, as protection against the wolf-pack's wiles, whenever they had reason to venture into the trees.

But the thought of the wolves was not the only thing that had made Ernst Tigelwurst shiver with fear.

Turning his face upwards, the carter stared over the edge of the pit and lifted his eyes towards the mountain which rose above the tree-tops, standing out in darker silhouette against the starlit sky. Ernst Tigelwurst shivered again. Although the night was chill, a tiny bead of sweat broke out on his forehead, trickled past his left eyebrow and hovered on his cheek. The carter brushed the droplet away, almost angrily, with the back of his hand. He gulped, swallowed hard, and gulped again as he peered up at the mountain. Halfway up the mountainside stood Alucard Castle – hidden for the moment, while the moon remained obscured behind the cloud, but Ernst Tigelwurst did not need to see the castle to know that it was there. Count Alucard lived in Alucard Castle. "Alucard" spelled "Dracula" backwards. Count Alucard, as every Tolokovin child sang in the schoolyard, was the Last of the dreaded Vampires . . .

"One – two – three, four, five,
Count Alucard eats boys alive.
Small girls too, if they're not good;
Bites their necks and drinks their blood—"

"What have you stopped for now?" Emil Gruff's sharp words broke in on Ernst Tigelwurst's thoughts. "Should I treat you like you treat your bullocks, carter, and crack a whip across your shoulders, in order to make you work?"

"No, Emil," replied Ernst Tigelwurst, with a firm shake of his head as a third shiver ran though him. And it was true. He did not need any further urging to get him to do what had to be done. The full moon peered out again, from behind the cloud, bathing the forest clearing in a silvery glow. And, although the

3

Transylvanian carter had feared the lengthy shadows while the moon's face had been hidden, the eerie light reminded him that vampires took to the skies when the moon was full.

"*Ter-Whooo-HOOOOO!*"

"Come on, Emil!" It was Ernst Tigelwurst's turn to do the urging. "Let's get this job finished and get home to our beds."

"*Swish-THUNK!*" . . . "*Swish-THUNK!*" . . . "*Swish-THUNK!*" . . . "*Swish-THUNK!*" . . .

The two men worked with a will and huge chunks of earth fairly flew now, from off their shovels, over the rim of the ever-deepening pit and on to the grassy floor.

"Mercy upon us!" Count Alucard sighed to himself, as he peered down over the castle's turreted roof,

through the tops of the tall fir trees, into the tiny forest clearing far below. "What are they up to this time?" he added, letting out a second sad little sigh. From so far away, he could make out no more than the stationary glow of the lantern on the rim of the pit – but Count Alucard knew to his cost that, if there were peasants in the forest after dark, then they could not be up to any good.

Count Alucard had first realised that something odd was happening about half an hour earlier that same night. The Count had not been able to sleep. Because he was vampire born, the Count was always a little edgy when there was a full moon in the sky. Lying in the comfort of his dark wood, satin-lined coffin, in the lowest castle dungeon, with a shaft of moonlight streaming in through the small, barred arched window high up on the dungeon wall, Count Alucard had been killing time by flicking, by candlelight, through the pages of the latest issue of *The Coffin-Maker's Journal* (his favourite magazine), when his sharp bat's hearing had picked up on a curious sound drifting from somewhere in the forest below.

"*Swish-THUNK!*" . . . "*Swish-THUNK!*" . . . "*Swish-THUNK!*" . . . "*Swish-THUNK!*" . . .

For several minutes, the Transylvanian vampire Count had tried his very hardest to concentrate his attention on an article, written by a New York undertaker, about the very latest in computerised fibre-glass coffins, which opened and closed silently by the lightest pressure on an internal button – but it had been no good, the strange sounds continued in his ears and, try as he might, he had been unable to ignore them.

Count Alucard had good reason to be worried. For

5

as long as he could remember, he had been tormented by the unwanted attentions of the villagers of Tolokovin. On several occasions, during his own lifetime, the peasants had stormed the castle and with one intention: to overpower the castle's occupant, hold him down, spread-eagled, on his own oak, ancient dining-table, and hammer a sharp-pointed wooden stake through his heart. Which would have been a cruel act, to say the very least, because Count Alucard – The Last of the Vampires – was as gentle a person as you might ever wish to come across on any dark and lonely night.

Unlike his ancestors, who were blood-drinking, scary, spooky creatures every one, Count Alucard was born a vegetarian vampire. Although, like all of the Alucards before him, the Count possessed the ability to turn himself into a bat during the hours of darkness – *he* changed into a fruit-eating bat on such occasions and had never been known to sink his pointy-teeth into anything other than a juicy peach, say, or a ripe, fleshy, purple plum. The very thought of biting a human being was enough to make Count Alucard cringe with horror. Whenever he was thirsty, the Count's favourite tipple was a full glass of tomato juice, tinkling with ice-cubes and heavily spiced, for preference, with Worcestershire Sauce.

Again, like his forebears, Count Alucard always dressed formally: black tail-coat and trousers; white stiff frilly-fronted shirt and neatly knotted white bow tie; black silk socks and black, well-polished shoes, and with a gold medallion (passed on to him by his father) suspended on a fine gold chain around his neck. Whenever and wherever he was out and about, either by day or night, the Count was never less than polite and helpful to anyone that he came across – and would never even dream of harming any living thing.

All of which goes some way to reveal the foolishness of the Tolokovinite peasants whose hatred for the occupant of the Castle Alucard was based entirely on old wives' tales and ancient superstitions.

"*Swish-THUNK!*" . . . "*Swish-THUNK!*" . . . "*Swish-THUNK!*" . . . "*Swish-THUNK!*" . . .

Unable to ignore the sounds, Count Alucard had clambered out of his coffin, slipped off his black, silk pyjamas (with the initials C.A. embroidered, in fine gold thread, on the jacket's breast pocket), dressed hastily and then sprinted, on his long, thin legs, out through the heavy oak door of the dungeon, up the several winding flights of worn stone steps and out on to the turreted flat roof.

Moments later, peering down at the glimmer of lantern light far, far below, Count Alucard was uncertain of what he ought to do? The "*Swish-THUNK!*" sounds of shovelling had stopped – or, if they were still going on, he could not hear them from his present distant height. Neither could his eyes make out any signs of movement? The vegetarian vampire puzzled in his mind for several seconds, wondering whether it was his duty to go down into the clearing and discover for himself what it was, exactly, that the intruders were up to?

Alas though, in spite of his vampire ancestry, the Count was a nervous sort of chap at heart. He could not count bravery among his list of attributes – if anything, he would be forced to describe himself as timid. Besides, he had no idea of how many intruders there

7

were in the forest clearing. The only thing that Count Alucard could be sure of, was that there was only one of him. A fact which, in itself, was enough to make him err on the side of caution rather than rush into anything.

He hesitated for so long, in fact, that as usually happens to those who cannot make their minds up, the situation was taken out of his hands. The glimmer of light from the clearing below, which had previously remained stationary, suddenly began to move. Count Alucard watched and waited several minutes more, as the orange glow flickered first, then set off, slowly meandering through the trees – sometimes visible, sometimes not – and down the mountain. The Count realised that the intruders must have completed whatever task they had set themselves in the forest clearing, and that now they were headed back towards Tolokovin.

It would be safe, the Transylvanian nobleman decided, for him to venture down as far as the clearing and find out what had been going on? Stepping up on to the parapet, Count Alucard took a firm grip on the hem of his scarlet-lined black cloak with both of his hands and stretched it out, on either side of his body. Then, without a second thought, he launched himself off the roof and out into the empty space beyond.

Count Alucard might not include himself among the most fearless of men, but there was one thing that did not bug him in the slightest: taking flight.

Having jumped off the roof, the vegetarian vampire seemed to hang for a moment, underneath the stars, his outspread cloak caught on the breeze that stirred in the topmost branches of the trees beneath him. And

8

then a curious thing happened. Still suspended on the gentle wind, Count Alucard appeared to tremble first, then shrivel quickly, clothes and all. A moment later, his human form had disappeared completely and in its place, hovering on wide, dark, outstretched membraneous wings was a tiny, furry-bodied creature with a snub-nosed face and sharp ears and pointy teeth. The Transylvanian nobleman had taken on his fruit-eating bat form.

Once he had accustomed himself to the soft night breeze, the Count beat his wings, rose first, then dipped and swooped down past the castle's grim walls. He then descended further still through the tree-tops, between the network of branches, into the forest clearing, which was bathed in moonlight. Count Alucard flattened out in flight and cruised across the clearing's length, skimming over the grass, then turned, zapped back again, a metre or thereabouts above level ground.

"How very odd?" the vegetarian vampire puzzled to himself as he cruised the clearing, searching in vain for any signs of the intruders' handiwork. But try as he might, and despite his bat's keen radar-like senses, he could not discover anything to signify that someone had recently been working there.

After having flown across the grassy surface several times, both East and West and North to South, and still without managing to come across the tell-tale signs of digging, Count Alucard gave up the search. He had decided that it was time to call a halt to the night's proceedings and that he would return when morning came and examine the area more thoroughly by daylight. Then, having taken that decision, he lifted his head towards the moon and, flitting between the branches, headed back toward where the castle's turreted roof stood out in black relief against the starlit sky.

Minutes later, having returned to human form, Count Alucard had changed back into his pyjamas and was stretched out in the satin-lined comfort of his polished, dark wood coffin, concentrating his attention on the article in *The Coffin-Maker's Journal* which had earlier caught his eye. "Although, taking one thing with another," he told himself, as he allowed his eyes to wander around the stone walls of the dungeon which were lit by the warm, golden, flickering glow of the huge candles in their cast-iron sconces, "I don't think that I would care for one of these computerised coffins – give me good old-fashioned Transylvanian home comforts every time."

Then, overcome by tiredness at last, the Count's eyelids dropped and the magazine fell from out of his slim fingers on to the stone-flagged floor.

"AH-ZZZZzzzzzzz . . ." Count Alucard was fast asleep. Because of his exertions in the forest, the Count was to sleep in much longer the following day than he had intended, an unintentional lapse which would cause him more adventures and excitements over the coming weeks, than dreams could ever provide him.

The wolves of Tolokovin were out and about at break of day the following morning, before the sun had crept over the mountain-top, spurred on partly by hunger but mostly by their own exuberance.

Boris, the grey-headed pack-leader led the way, loping eagerly along but ever-mindful that he must not step up the pace beyond the reach of the smallest of the wolves. The wise old wolf moved through the trees with sure-footed ease – Boris knew every dip and fold in that wide-ranging forest as well as he knew every hair on his own battle-scarred flea-bitten haunches. He knew, almost by instinct, which of the forest trails were safe to travel along and which were the ones that had been made by human feet and were therefore to be avoided.

Mikhail and Lubka, two fully grown, sleek-furred male wolves, followed close on Boris's tail, eager to prove to the rest of the pack that they were stronger and faster than any others. When the time would finally arrive, as arrive it surely must, for a new pack-leader to succeed Boris, then that honour would belong to whichever of the pair could beat the other in fair fight.

For the time being though, the two pretenders to the pack-leader's title were content to sprint along, as friends, shoulder to shoulder and at Boris's heels. Behind Mikhail and Lubka raced the main body of wolves: Ivan, Karl, Olga, Tanya, Krupkin, Babushka,

Brelka and all the rest – the females shepherding the younger wolves and doling out a cautionary nip for any cub that showed an inclination to stray from the pack, either to the left or to the right. Bringing up the rear, some several metres behind the rest, Stefan, one of the pack-elders, kept a wary look-out to make sure there were no stragglers.

As the wolf-pack broke from cover and headed towards the forest clearing which lay beneath the castle, Boris raised his eyes towards Count Alucard's ancestral home which rose up out of the early-morning mist. Sometimes, when the wolf-pack frolicked close by Alucard Castle, the Transylvanian nobleman came out and joined them at their play. Occasionally, if the wolves were out and about at night, the Count assumed his bat form and flitted to-and-fro, over Boris's head, as the wolf-pack roamed through the moonlit trees.

Feared and despised by the people of Tolokovin, Count Alucard led a lonely life in his castle – he counted on the wolves for companionship and considered each and every member of the pack his friend. The Count called the wolves his "children of the night", and while he would have done his very best to see that no harm came to any one of them, in return the wolves would have protected the Count, with tooth and claw, against any danger that might chance along.

There was no sign of Count Alucard however, on that particular morning. The Count was fast asleep now as the wolves approached, safe and snug in his polished coffin. Boris, realising that they were not going to enjoy the Count's company on that occasion, but unaware of the reason why, veered off to the right as the clearing came into view. The old wolf led his pack back towards the shelter of the forest, for while the open space was a safe enough place for the cubs to romp around in when Count Alucard was present; the Count's absence gave Boris sufficient reason to look elsewhere for a resting place.

In seconds the wolf-pack was out of sight again, hidden by the trees – with the exception of one of its members. Skopka, a young male wolf, had fallen far behind the others. Skopka's dalliance had not given Stefan, the "straggler-watcher" any cause for concern. Skopka, after all, was no mere cub, he was a half-grown wolf, big for his years, and capable, or so Stefan had judged, of looking after himself and able to catch up with the pack again when he felt like doing so. But Stefan had not been aware of the fact that Skopka had a sharp thorn in his left fore-paw. By the time the pack had approached the clearing, Skopka had fallen so far behind as to be completely out of sight.

When Skopka limped into the clearing, there was no sign to hint at where the others had gone? Of course, if the young wolf had had his wits about him, he would have picked up the wolf-scent all too easily. But Skopka was distracted by the pain in his paw. Similarly, if he had not been bothered by the thorn, the solitary wolf would surely have noticed the trap that Emil Gruff, the woodcutter, and Ernst Tigelwurst, the carter, had set in the clearing. The sparse covering of branches, twigs, leaves and grass, which the two Tolokovinites had spread over the pit was plain enough for any to see.

But Skopka was not looking where he was going as

he moved across the open ground. Instinct told the wolf that he was foolish to venture out, alone, from the safety of the trees. It had been some time now since he had last had contact with the pack, and his fears were mounting. In an attempt to catch up with the others, unaware that they had veered off in another direction, Skopka decided to suffer the pain in his paw and to pick up speed. It was the wolf's bad luck that he should choose the very moment when the hidden pit lay directly ahead, to break into a clumsy run.

With both of his front legs stretched out in front of him, Skopka's forepaws struck the flimsy covering of the pit together. Feeling the ground give way beneath him, Skopka scrabbled, wildly, with all four paws at once, as he crashed through the leaves and twigs and fell, in a heap, on the earth below. Unhurt but puzzled, the young wolf rolled over and on to his feet. He stared up at where the morning sunlight filtered through the hole he had made in the flimsy network above his head. Again on instinct, Skopka threw back his head and let out a mournful howl:

"Ah-whooo-OOOOOOH!"

At the same time as the cry broke from his throat, the young wolf's nose picked up the man-scent that was all around him. Caution told Skopka that he would do better to hold his silence. For the moment at least, he did not let out another sound. The four earth walls that contained him, he now recognised, had been fashioned by human hands. Not only that, but one of the two separate "man-smells" in Skopka's nostrils was the same pungent scent that betrayed the presence of the steel-jawed traps that he often skirted in the forest.

It was Emil Gruff, the woodcutter, who was fond of setting traps (strong enough to snap a young wolf's leg in two) on the forest trails. Emil Gruff hated wolves. Skopka did not know that the woodcutter's name was Emil Gruff, but he knew enough to recognise the scent that the woodcutter gave off. Neither could the young wolf guess at what kind of madness would possess two humans to make them choose to dig a useless hole in a forest clearing, then cover it with leaves and branches. But humankind, as Skopka knew well, was up to all manner of madnesses. There was one thing that the young wolf could be sure of, if the woodcutter had a hand in the matter, then there would be some sort of evil lurking in his purpose.

Gazing up again, through the hole he had made when he had crashed through the covering, Skopka wondered, but without much hope, whether he might be able to leap up and out of his earthen prison? Anything was worth a try. Settling himself back on his haunches, the young wolf summoned his strength and tensed his muscles, then thrust his body upwards, front legs outstretched. His front paws, alas, fell sufficiently short of the pit's rim for Skopka to realise that escape did not lie in that direction. It was as if it suddenly occurred to him that the two humans had dug the pit with the very intention of trapping a wolf alive.

Skopka, preserving his strength, settled himself on the earth floor. When his fellow wolves realised that he was missing, they would come back to look for him. When Skopka sensed the vibration of the pack's feet as they pounded through the forest, or, if the wind was in the right direction, when he got the first whiff of their approaching scent, *then* he would let out a howl to let

15

them know exactly where to find him. He did not know how the wolves would help him get out of the hole, but clever old Boris would think of something. Clever old Boris always thought of something. Clever old Boris could come up with a solution to every problem.

If, on the other hand, the humans returned before the wolves . . . well, if that were to prove the case, the young wolf reasoned to himself, he would just have to deal with that situation when it arose.

Lying outstretched on the floor of the pit, Skopka settled his nose between his forelegs and began to whimper, softly.

One thing gave him some light comfort: the thorn in his foot which had been troubling him seemed to have worked itself free.

2

"Heavens above!" murmured Count Alucard, the vegetarian vampire, as he sat up in his coffin, blinking at the light. "I must have overslept."

The candles in the tall, cast-iron, scroll-worked sconces, had flickered out long hours before. A bright shaft of sunlight, streaming in through the high arched window, had moved slowly down the opposite dungeon wall and, with the midday sun now high in the sky, had come to rest on the open coffin. It had been this bright beam of light, caressing the Count's pale cheeks, that had aroused him from his slumbers.

Count Alucard did not usually sleep in late. Unlike his forebears, who had been blood-drinking monsters every single one, Count Alucard was an early riser. True vampires (as anyone who knows anything at all about such night-time creatures knows) are nocturnal things by nature. Shunning sunlight, they spend the day-time hours inside their coffins and with the heavy coffin lid shut tight, emerging only when the world is dark. But Count Alucard, being a vegetarian vampire, had long, long ago decided that the ways of other vampires did not suit him.

"Drink up your nice glass of blood, son, before you go downstairs and clamber into your coffin," his

17

father, the previous Count Alucard, had often urged him as they had taken breakfast together in the ancient castle's draughty, vaulted, dining-hall. But even as a boy, the young Alucard had turned his nose up at the treats which other vampires relished. "I don't know who you take after, lad – it must be your mother's side of the family, for it certainly isn't mine!" the old Count used to exclaim, with a bewildered shake of his head, unable to fathom his own son's fads and fancies. Then, after the sun was up and his father fast asleep in the comforting darkness of his own coffin, the young Alucard had regularly tiptoed from the dungeon that was his nursery, up the steep stone steps, brushing aside the cobwebs, out through the castle's creaking front door and into the sunlight. Once there, he would frolic in the trees, nibble on blackberries, redcurrants and other fruits of the forest – and pick wild flowers.

Long years later, with the old Count Alucard's body now laid to rest in the family vault, among the bones of his vampirical ancestors, the son had grown into the man and had succeeded to his father's title. The present Count Alucard was able to lead the life which suited him best, with no one now to question what he ate or how he passed his time. He could choose for himself what time of night or day he went outside the castle, without fear of anyone scolding him. But although he still loved to feel the sun on his face, and to lie on his back and watch white, fleecy clouds scudding across a bright blue sky, he also enjoyed the moonlight hours which he spent zapping through the Forest of Tolokovin on bat-wings, in the good company of the wolves, his "children of the night".

Another part of the Count that had stayed true to his vampire roots, was the manner in which he chose to sleep. For whether he took his rest by day or night, and no matter where he travelled around the world, he much preferred to sleep in a coffin rather than a bed. "I cannot imagine why it is," he often said, "but I simply cannot get a good night's rest in a bed – I just toss and turn all night." If you should chance to come across him, on his travels, and were able to pluck up sufficient courage to suggest to him that sleeping in a coffin was a spooky way of going on, Count Alucard would shrug his thin shoulders and spread his pale hands apart, palms upward, and say: "It takes all sorts to make a world," followed by, "Live and let live."

On that particular morning, when the Count had overslept and after he had been awakened by the sunlight stealing across his face, he sat up, yawned, stretched his arms, dangled a long leg over the side of his coffin, felt with his foot for the stone floor of his cell then, after his big toe had encountered coldness, despatched his other leg to join the first. After dressing leisurely and still puzzling over the previous night's mysterious happenings, Count Alucard took himself out of the castle and wandered down as far as the clearing. What he discovered there served only to puzzle him more.

He had, he felt sure, on his moonlit bat's flight, covered every square metre of the clearing and found nothing to suggest that anyone had been at work with a shovel. Now, as he sauntered out through the fringe of trees, it was immediately obvious to him where the previous night's skulduggery had taken place. A gaping hole, about a metre and a half across and three

19

metres long, was plainly visible at the far end of the clearing. But how could he not have spotted it the last time he had been there? Admittedly, it had been dark at the time, but he had skimmed so close to the ground, and searched the area so thoroughly, it seemed impossible that he could have failed to notice such a large hole in the ground? And why, he also asked himself, would anyone want to waste their time, in the middle of the night, in digging such a pit? Unless, of course, they had intended to bury something . . . or some *body*? For it had all at once occurred to Count Alucard that the hole looked rather like a large open grave.

"Saint Unfortunato save us!" gasped the Count. He shivered as he contemplated the horrifying possibility. Transylvanian vampire he might be, and well might he dwell all alone in a spooky castle, nevertheless the very idea of a dead body on his own doorstep, so to speak, was enough to cause him goosebumps around the back of his neck and pins-and-needles all along his spine.

"Ah-wher-wher-wher-wher-wherrrrrrr!"

The solitary whimpering of a single wolf, somewhere close at hand, broke in on the vegetarian vampire's thoughts, providing him with an even worse possibility to consider? "Oh, my word!" the Count murmured to himself. "Supposing some poor creature has fallen down into that pit, during the night, and can't get out? It really is *the* most ridiculous place to leave a hole untended, for any stray animal to tumble into in the dark." For Count Alucard was such a trusting kind-hearted fellow that it did not so much as cross his mind that the pit had been dug with that very intention.

"Ah-wher-wher-wher-wher-wherrrrrr!"

There was another whimper, similar to the first, and the Count, deciding that his last fear had been confirmed, strode off immediately across the clearing. Arriving at the edge of the pit, he leaned forwards and peered down. But it seemed to him as if the hole was empty, unless there was an animal hidden, trembling, underneath the quantity of sticks and grass and twigs and leaves that were strewn across the bottom.

"Ah-wher-wher-wher-wher-wherrrrrr!"

"Hello?" called the Count, squinting down into the hole. "Is there something down there?"

But there was neither sound nor movement coming from underneath the foliage on the floor of the pit, and Count Alucard told himself that the whimpering must be coming from another direction. It was at that moment that the undergrowth stirred, at the edge of the forest, and a lone female wolf crept out of the trees, head low, ears flattened and cowering with her belly brushing the ground.

"Ah-wher-wher-wher-wher-wherrrrr!" whined the wolf – the Count was no longer in any doubt as to where the sound had been coming from.

Standing quite still, Count Alucard watched as the wolf, her tail between her legs, stole across the clearing and in his direction, twitching her nose urgently as she sniffed at the grass. Ignoring the Count completely, indeed, she behaved as if she hadn't even seen him, the she-wolf inched her way to the edge of the pit where, after sniffing her way all round the rim, she settled herself full-length on the ground, motionless, but making the same whimpering sounds as before.

"Ah-wher-wher-wher-wher-wherrrrrrr!"

"What is it, Valentina?" asked the Count, crossing to where the wolf was lying and addressing her by name. "What's wrong, old girl?" he continued, squatting and stroking the animal's flanks. "Why aren't you with the rest of the pack? And where's young Skopka – he's not usually far from your side?"

"Ah-whoo-OOOOOOH!"

At the very mention of the missing wolf, Valentina lifted her head and let out a long, low mournful howl. Skopka was the she-wolf's son – not only that, but was the only cub to have survived, two years before, from a litter of triplets; the she-cub of that trio having died at birth, the second male cub having perished in one of Emil Gruff's despicable steel-jawed traps. It was no wonder then, that Valentina usually ran close to Skopka, seldom letting the half-grown male wolf stray far from her sight.

In those same moments, as Valentina threw back her head and let out that despairing howl, a terrible thought flashed through the vegetarian vampire's mind. He had suddenly realised what had really happened. The hole that had been dug during the previous night had been intended as an animal-trap. The leaves and branches, now scattered across the floor of the pit, had been used to cover up the trap, which was why he had not seen it during his night-time search. But, worst of all, the trap had claimed Skopka as its victim. But *why* had the young wolf been kidnapped, Count Alucard asked himself and, more importantly, where had his kidnappers taken him?

Before the Transylvanian nobleman could ponder further on the vexing problem of where Skopka had been taken, there was a sudden stirring in the under-growth at the edge of the forest and then Boris leaped out and into the clearing. Close on the pack-leader's heels, as always, raced Mikhail and Lubka, nose to nose, with the rest of the wolf-pack bounding along in close formation and not far behind. Just as Valentina had come back in search of Skopka, so had the other wolves returned to look for Valentina and followed her scent.

Moments later, all of the wolves were gathered around the rim of the pit, some of them sniffing anx-iously at the ground, others nuzzling Valentina's flanks, seemingly aware and understanding of her loss, while several pack-members, squatting on their haunches, raised their heads and bayed, fretfully, at the clear blue sky. While all of this was going on, Boris padded across to where the Count was standing and nuzzled his nose into the vegetarian vampire's hand.

"Yes, Boris," Count Alucard murmured, his fingers folding gently around the pack-leader's jaws. "I know that something bad has happened to Skopka. Believe me, I intend to go and rescue him and bring him back. But at this moment, I do not know who it is that has taken him; neither do I have the first idea of where I might begin to look. If I am to find him, old friend, I shall need your help."

In answer, Boris panted, urgently, his tongue lolling out at one side of his mouth. The old wolf did not know what it was that he would have to do, but he was eager to make a start.

"Can't you make these wretched beasts go any faster, Ernst Tigelwurst?" grumbled Police Sergeant

Alphonse Kropotel, perched up on the driving-seat of the bullock-cart, squashed between the carter and Emil Gruff, the woodcutter. Then, after glancing up at the darkening sky, the Tolokovin police officer peered nervously into the lengthening shadows in the tall fir trees which surrounded them on every side. "It will be night-time in an hour or so," he added.

Ernst Tigelwurst was concentrating on guiding his bullocks along the twisting cart-track and ignored the policeman's words, but Emil Gruff let out a little snigger, and said: "What's the matter, sergeant? Are you afraid of the dark?"

"Ah-Whoooo-HOOOOOOOO!"

Skopka, locked inside the close confines of the iron-barred cage on the back of the cart, lifted his head towards the gradually appearing moon and let out a fretful howl. The spooky sound affected even the

woodcutter who spent his every working hour inside the forest, and his hands closed around the haft of his gleaming axe which lay across his knees. Sergeant Kropotel shivered, ran a nervous forefinger around the inside of his uniform collar and then took out a red handkerchief with white spots and mopped several beads of sweat from off his brow.

"Up, Osman! *Pull*, Ludwig!" Ernst Tigelwurst commanded his bullocks. At the same time, he raised his long whip above his head and flicked it out across the noses of the huge beasts which were straining in the shafts.

In answer to these urgings, the bullocks made a sudden extra effort and the cart moved faster. Then, as the front wheel lumbered over a deep rut in the forest track, the cart lurched violently, causing the three men to bounce on the hard wooden seat.

"Ouch!" said Sergeant Kropotel, and added: "Can't you drive with a little more care?"

"I can't drive with more care *and* drive faster," growled Tigelwurst. "You can have either speed or comfort, Sergeant Kropotel, but you can't have both. Either make up your mind which one you want, or save your breath until supper-time to cool your goat's-meat soup."

The only thing that Sergeant Kropotel really wanted, at that moment, was to be out of the forest, but as that was not possible, he took the carter's advice and held his tongue. As both Ernst Tigelvurst and Emil Gruff were surly men not given much to conversation, the journey continued for quite some time without a word being said. Skopka, deciding not to show to his captors that he was both uncomfortable and afraid, settled himself, as best he could, on the iron-barred cold floor of his cage, and made not so much as another whimper. The only sounds to be heard, as the cart travelled along the forest track, were the creaking of the huge wooden wheels and the panting of the bullocks as they laboured in the shafts.

Despite the animals' extra efforts, progress was slow. The narrow, twisting path through the trees had been tricky enough to negotiate during the day, but in the failing light of evening, manoeuvring the clumsy cart was an even harder task.

They had been on the move for almost twelve hours. The woodcutter and the carter had returned to the clearing at dawn that morning. Delighted at finding that their trap had worked, they had manhandled the captive out of the pit with the aid of a net and secured it in the cage on the back of the cart. Having then met up with the unscrupulous Alphonse Kropotel, they had set off at first light along the forest cart-track – but there was still no sign, all these long hours later, that their journey was nearing an end.

The Forests of Tolokovin were wide-ranging. If viewed from the top of Tolokovin Mountain, the thickly wooded trees spread out, in every direction as far as the eye could see. Many a luckless traveller, according to local legend, setting out to cross the forest, had entered the trees on one side, but never emerged from an opposite end.

Both Ernst Tigelwurst and Alphonse Kropotel were anxious in case night should fall and they might lose their way in the forest, while even Emil Gruff who, after all, made his living in the forest, was not without misgivings, for they were travelling through an area of the forest which he had never before ventured into.

"I only hope that what you have promised us is true, Sergeant Kropotel," growled the woodcutter, nodding over his shoulder at Skopka as he turned his thoughts to other matters, "and that when we *do* arrive at the edge of the forest, the mysterious foreigner that you spoke of will be waiting there to take that animal off our hands."

"Of course it's true," snapped Kropotel, rubbing his hands together greedily. "*And* he'll be more than willing to reward us handsomely for bringing him the wolf. Why else would I have suggested that you trap the beast, except to put money in our pockets?"

"It sounds too good to be true," said Ernst Tigelwurst, scratching at the spot between his shoulder-blades where a lively flea had recently taken up residence. "Why would anyone pay out good money for a mangy Transylvanian wolf?"

"Take whatever cash is offered you and ask questions afterwards," Alphonse Kropotel replied. "Foreigners are curious folk at the best of times – I've known them turn their noses up at goose-grease broth and delicious goat's-gristle stew—" The police sergeant broke off and again glanced fearfully at the ever-darkening sky, then shivered. "Saint Unfortunato preserve us," he murmured, "if we don't get out of this forest before nightfall."

"*Ter-Whoooo-HOOOOOOOO!*"

As if to underline Alphonse Kropotel's misgivings, an owl, perched high in a tall fir tree, had fluttered its wings then hooted, heralding approaching night.

"Faster, Ludwig! Heave, Osman!" cried Ernst Tigelwurst, urging the straining bullocks to even greater effort as he cracked his whip above the tips of their horns.

Boris, the wily leader of the Tolokovin wolf-pack, had found little difficulty in picking up the scent, despite the fact that several hours must have elapsed since the bullock-cart had passed that way. Tongue lolling and head stretched eagerly forward, he trotted along the forest track at an easy pace. Indeed, the old wolf might easily have travelled through the forest at ten times his present speed, were it not for the fact that he had contained his pace so that Count Alucard might follow, at a jog-trot, in his wake.

The Transylvanian nobleman and his animal friend had been making steady progress. They had been on the trail of the bullock-cart all that afternoon and early evening, stopping every now and then for the Count to regain his breath. But while the vegetarian vampire guessed that they were probably moving faster than the clumsy vehicle they were pursuing – which would be travelling slowly along the tortuously twisting track – he also realised that the villains who had kidnapped Skopka had got several hours start on him and, unless he could increase his pace, there was small chance of his catching up with them for several days. Except that Count Alucard had an ace kept up his sleeve.

"Easy, Boris! Rest, rest, old friend!" gasped the Count, bringing his long legs to another halt. Then, placing his slim hands on his hips, he peered up through the network of branches at where the very first star of that evening twinkled down from the ever-darkening sky. "The night has come at last," panted Count Alucard, still struggling to catch his breath.

"And that means that we can *really* put on some speed!"

Boris, seeming to understand the Count's meaning, squatted on his haunches, staring up into the vegetarian vampire's face and anticipating what was about to happen. For, as the old wolf knew, when darkness fell, Count Aluard's vampirical powers allowed him to turn himself into a bat. Although Boris had watched this transformation take place a hundred times and more, it never ceased to astonish and delight him and he was always eager to see it happen again.

Planting his feet firmly, wide apart and in the centre of the cart-track, Count Alucard reached down, grasped the hem of his scarlet-lined black cloak with both of his hands then spread them out on either side of his slim body. Then, watched keenly by Boris who had his head cocked on one side, the vegetarian vampire stood quite still for several seconds before taking a deep breath and tightly shutting his eyes. The Count's body seemed to tremble and suddenly began to shrink, growing smaller and smaller, faster and faster, like a deflating balloon.

A split second later, Count Alucard seemed to have disappeared altogether and, hovering on widespread wing in the place where he had stood, was a small, furry-bodied, snub-nosed, sharp-toothed, black-eyed, ears-pricked bat. The transformation from Transylvanian nobleman to fruit-eating bat was complete.

"Ah-WHOOOOO-HOOOoooooooh!"

Boris craned his neck, lifted his head, bared his teeth and howled excitedly at the pale moon which had just appeared in a patch of sky directly over the spot where the two of them were placed. Then, knowing exactly what was expected of him, the old wolf sprang off his haunches and on to his paws, sprinting off along the forest track. At the same moment the black bat flapped its outspread parchment-like wings, rose first, then dipped, and settling into easy flight, flitted between the lower branches of the forest trees.

As the night sky turned from deepest blue to velvet black, and a thousand stars emerged to twinkle in the Transylvanian sky, the Tolokovin wolf pack-leader bounded eagerly along the cart-track, through the forest, and with his friend, Count Alucard, flitting overhead and never straying far from the old wolf's head.

"At this rate," the vegetarian vampire told himself, as he scudded along on outstretched wing, "we should reach the other side of the forest within the hour." But a smaller and more cautious voice inside his head remembered the start that their quarry had on them, and he was already wondering whether one hour might not be soon enough.

3

"Good! Right on time," growled the greedy police sergeant, Alphonse Kropotel with grim satisfaction, as he watched the helicopter hover over the bleak Transylvanian wasteland, close by the edge of the forest, before making its final descent inside the ring of flickering lanterns which the three Tolokovinites had previously laid out to mark the landing area. Then, as the private aircraft came closer, the three men covered their ears against the roar of the engines and crouched close to the ground as the down-draught from the rotor-blades flattened the thick grass all around them.

Inside the iron-barred cage, still tied to the rear of the bullock-cart and unprotected against the noise and the buffeting of the wind, Skopka cowered and blinked in the glare of the searchlights on the helicopter's underbelly, and trembled yet again with fear.

"Don't hand the animal over until they've given us the money," advised Emil Gruff as the aircraft's engines were switched off.

"As if I would!" snapped Alphonse Kropotel.

"And be sure to count the money first," counselled Ernst Tigelwurst, "to make sure that every grobek is there."

"Of course I'll count the money – do you take me for a fool!" replied the policeman. "Come on," he added, rising to his feet as two men, in flying denims, clambered from the helicopter and ran towards them. "Let's get this task over and done with." Then, with his two henchmen in close attendance, Alphonse Kropotel stroke across to meet the approaching helicopter crewmen.

Still hugging the floor of his cage, Skopka peered across at where, in the pale light of the moon, the group of men were talking in urgent whispers. Although he had no idea of what was going on, judging by the glances that were constantly being turned in his direction, the young wolf guessed that he was the subject of that conversation. He wondered, without a great deal of hope, whether providing him with food and drink might be on their agenda. From the moment that he had been manhandled, roughly and by means of a net, out of the forest pit and into the cage, he had not been given a morsel of food or even a sip of water. The hunger pangs, gnawing in his belly, were bad enough, but his need for a drink was worse. His tongue was dry inside his mouth. Just for a moment, Skopka toyed with the thought of throwing back his head, opening his jaws, and giving vent to a full-throttled howl for help. He dismissed the idea as quickly as it had occurred to him. Animal common sense told him that his long day's journey in captivity had take him far too far from his home territories for any cry for help to reach the ears of the Tolokovin pack, and if there was not a friendly wolf for miles around, who else could he possibly expect to come to his assistance? Skopka chose instead to put his jowls on the ground, push his nose through the bars of his prison and display his misery by whining softly.

Then, just at the moment when his spirits were at their lowest ebb, a familiar voice spoke to him out of the shadows.

"Easy, Skopka! Take heart, my young friend."

"Ah-wher-wher-wher-wher-WHOOOO!"

Instantly aware of Count Alucard's friendly presence, the young wolf had sprung up on all fours and let out a joyful welcoming yelp. The sudden sound caused both the bullocks to fidget in the cart-shafts and moan uneasily, drawing the attentions of the men.

"What was that?" asked the taller of the helicopter's crewmen, peering across suspiciously towards the cart. But Skopka, realising his mistake, did not utter another sound and the bullocks settled down again.

"It was nothing," said Ernst Tigelwurst with a shrug. "Perhaps a stoat or a weasel ran under the bellies of the beasts, disturbing them. Bullocks are nervous creatures at the best of times."

"Who could blame them?" asked Emil Gruff, glancing fearfully out at the dark forbidding wasteland. "Who wouldn't be nervous in a Godforsaken place like this?"

"Let's get our business over quickly," said Alphonse Kropotel to the taller of the two crewmen. "Have you got the money?"

"Not so fast," replied the tall man, whose name was Captain Roth. "Your money's safe in here," he added. "And it's yours – but not until you've helped us load the animal on to the 'copter."

"Not so fast yourself. We need to count those grobeks first," snapped Kropotel. Then, turning to the woodcutter, he pointed across at the flickering lanterns they had laid out as landing lights. "Fetch one of those Emil, so that we can make sure the money's all here."

Moments later, when the only sounds to be heard were the voices of the three Tolokovinites as they greedily counted and recounted the bundles of grobeks, Count Alucard's head appeared over the side of the bullock-cart and he whispered at the captive wolf. "Quietly does it this time, Skopka," he cautioned. "And I'll have you out of there in no time." But any hopes that the Count might have had of setting the young wolf free and stealing off into the darkness of the night were dashed immediately. The door to the cage was securely fastened with a stout brass lock.

"Botheration!" the vegetarian vampire murmured to himself, for there was no way that he could release Skopka without a hacksaw or the key.

Count Alucard turned his eyes in another direction. He looked over at the edge of the forest, peering at the spot in the undergrowth where he knew that Boris, the faithful leader of the Tolokovin wolf-pack lay, obediently concealed exactly where the Count had told him to stay. For a moment or two, the Transylvanian nobleman toyed with the idea of summoning Boris to his side, then charging out of the darkness with the old wolf and putting the group of men to flight. After all, the Count assured himself, although they were outnumbered, at least they would have surprise on their side. But the vegetarian vampire dismissed the thought.

While Boris was a brave-hearted wolf whose

courage could not be faulted, he was well past his fighting days. Besides, the Count told himself, for all he knew the men he had to deal with might well be armed. No, he would need to resort to cunning, rather than bravery, if he was going to rescue Skopka. Then, having arrived at his decision, Count Alucard composed his mind and thought hard.

"Good!" exclaimed Alphonse Kropotel, snapping shut the briefcase. "The money's all here, every grobek. It only remains to put the wolf on to the helicopter and we can go our separate ways."

"Oh, deary-dear!" sighed Count Alucard, as he realised that the five men were striding out towards him. "He who hesitates is lost," he added. For, while he had been pondering how best to tackle the situation, the situation had overtaken him. The wolf-nappers had settled their business. There was no time now for the vegetarian vampire to do anything – except run away.

"Don't worry, Skopka," the Count whispered hastily through the bars of the cage. "I'm not going far. I won't desert you. Wherever you're being taken, I shall go there too." With which, and as the three Tolokovinites and the helicopter's crewmen drew closer, the Count ducked his head and stumbled awkwardly away, half-crouching, towards the shelter of the forest.

"Does it bite?" asked the shorter of the crewmen, as the group arrived at the bullock-cart, and he peered anxiously through the bars of the cage. Cheered by Count Alucard's appearance, Skopka had stopped cowering and was now staring with some defiance at his captors.

"Put your fingers through the bars," suggested Ernst Tigelwurst with a snigger, "and you'll find out for yourself."

"No, thank you," replied the crewman, with a shiver. His name was Albert Hoffmeyer, he had a pointed black beard, wore glasses with thick lenses and he was the helicopter's navigator.

"It's a mangy-looking brute," said Sergeant Kropotel, twisting the ends of his moustache with fingers and thumbs. "I can't imagine why anyone would want to waste good money on such a miserable specimen?"

"That is for our employer to know, and for you to find out," said Captain Roth, with a shrug. "And now, if you will give us a hand to get the animal on board, we'll take our leave of you. We've dawdled here too long already."

Ernst Tigelwurst scrambled up on to the back of his cart and shoved at the cage while the other four men tugged it closer to the edge. Then "Heave!" said Alphonse Kropotel as they manhandled the iron-barred cage and the captive wolf up on to their shoulders.

"Watch your fingers!" said Tigelwurst to the navigator, with a wink at Emil Gruff. Albert Hoffmeyer gulped, shifted his grip on the cage and blinked, nervously, through his glasses.

Their heavy burden, coupled with the uneven grass-clumped ground beneath their feet, caused the five men to walk unsteadily as they crossed, puffing and panting, to where the helicopter waited in the pale glow of the flickering lanterns.

"Go home, Boris. Go back, old friend," and, as he

36

spoke, Count Alucard tugged gently at the loose folds of skin under the old wolf's jowls. "Go back to Tolokovin – there is nothing more that you can do. You have come as far as it is possible, while my journeying has only just begun." With which, the vegetarian vampire gave the pack-leader a friendly farewell slap across his haunches then watched as Boris loped off, back the way that they had first come, along the forest track which led back to the wolf-pack's home territories.

As the old wolf disappeared into the dark night of the forest, the Count, still hidden in the undergrowth, turned his attention back to the wasteland beyond. The cage, containing Skopka, had been loaded into the helicopter some minutes before. Captain Roth and Albert Hoffmeyer, the navigator, were seated in the cockpit, ready for take-off. The Tolokovin trio (Alphonse Kropotel, Ernst Tigelwurst and Emil Gruff) had set off aboard the bullock-cart some moments before and were headed, their business completed, not back towards their hometown, but off in the opposite direction. With luck, they hoped to find an all-night tavern where they could split the spoils they carried in the briefcase, and celebrate their good fortune.

There was a steady *Whirr*, as the helicopter's engines were switched on, and then the rotor-blades began to turn – slowly at first, then faster and increasing in sound, causing the grass to flatten all around the aircraft.

Still in the shelter of the forest's edge, Count Alucard rose to his feet, took hold of the hem of his scarlet-lined black cloak then spread his arms on either side of his body. For the second time that night, the Count became his bat-self. Then, as the helicopter began to rise, the vegetarian vampire took off too, zapping across to where the helicopter hovered, several metres above the ground, while Captain Roth steered its nose towards the direction he intended to take.

Buffetted by the down-draught from the rotor-blades, the Count found shelter underneath the helicopter's hull. Once there, and as the aircraft continued to hover, the vegetarian vampire bat took a firm grip with his needle-sharp claws around a metal bar which held in place the spotlight on the aircraft's underbelly. Snug and protected by the undercarriage and hanging upside-down, he wrapped his membraneous wings around his furry black body and held on tight. Eyes closed, and fast asleep in seconds, the Count was unaware of the sudden swift upsurge as the helicopter rose high above the ground, then sped away, through a skein of scudding black clouds, into the star-studded night sky and off in the direction from whence it had first arrived.

"Mission accomplished," said Captain Roth, with a grin, as the helicopter gained both speed and height.

"Not quite, captain," replied Albert Hoffmeyer, the navigator, glancing over his shoulder at where Skopka lay contained in the cage in the aircraft's hold. "Not until we've got that wretched beast from off our hands." Then, wrinkling his nose distastefully, he added: "Pooh! It stinks to high heaven!"

"Of course it stinks, it's a wolf," said the helicopter pilot, with a shrug. "All wolves stink. It's the nature of the beast. You'd stink yourself if you spent your life skulking in the dark of the undergrowth in the forest. But all that will change for him when he gets to his new home. He'll wonder at how his luck has changed: fresh meat provided every day; a bowl of water set down for him; and a nice, clean cage for him to prowl up and down in to his heart's content for the rest of his days. He's got it made, has Mister Wolf. No more worries for that one, eh?"

"I suppose you're right, captain," agreed Albert Hoffmeyer. "A life of idleness to be envied."

It was lucky for Skopka that he could not understand a word of what was being said. The young wolf had more than enough to worry about already, without adding to his troubles. Lying on the floor of his uncomfortable cage, Skopka could see through the helicopter's open hatch that he was being transported across the sky. Skopka had never before risen higher above solid ground than that short distance that his own four legs could take him – jumping over a fallen log, for instance, or leaping across a clump of bracken in the forest. The young wolf was not the sort of animal to take fright easily, but the strange sensation of travelling through thin air was not something with which he could easily come to terms. If he had also been expected to accept the fact that all the future held for him was a lifetime in captivity, it might have been too much for him to take.

As things stood, unaware of what tomorrow might bring, Skopka shivered nervously as he lay outstretched, and continued to stare through the helicopter's open hatchway at the tops of the trees which were a long, long way beneath him – and getting further away with each passing second.

There was, however, one bright shining ray of hope on an otherwise dark horizon. Skopka still treasured, inside his head, the reassuring words that his friend Count Alucard, had whispered at him just before he had been manhandled inside the helicopter. The young wolf knew that the Count would not let him down. He guessed that, even now, Count Alucard was not far away, and as long as he had the Transylvanian nobleman to rely on, Skopka, the young wolf from the Tolokovin pack, took comfort in the knowledge that he was not entirely alone.

Protected from the blustery night winds by the helicopter's undercarriage, snugly wrapped up inside his own parchment-like wings, the vampire bat hung upside-down and fast asleep. Having spent the entire previous day in his pursuit of Skopka, the Count was very tired. So tired, in fact, that he had no difficulty whatsoever in slumbering soundly, hanging upside-down and suspended underneath the helicopter which had now levelled out and was cruising over open countryside.

Stars twinkled motionless in the vast, black sky overhead, while the glimmering lights of the towns and many villages came and slipped away below as the helicopter passed over them. Count Alucard was unaware of this. When the aircrfat arrived at its eventual destination (wherever that might be?) it would be time for the vegetarian vampire-bat to rouse itself from sleep. But for the time being at least, Count Alucard was grateful for whatever rest might come his way . . .

"Well done, captain!" said Albert Hoffmeyer, as the helicopter's wheels touched gently on the ground. "Nice landing!"

"Home again," said Captain Roth, acknowledging his navigator's congratulations with a modest shrug. Then, leaning forward, the pilot flicked the switch which would bring the helicopter's rotor-blades to a halt.

Behind the two-man crew, in the cramped iron cage in the aircraft's hold, Skopka's ears pricked. Animal sense told the young wolf that he was safely back on solid ground. He was grateful for the security this knowledge brought him and, at the same time, nervous as to what would happen to him next! Skopka had not closed his eyes, indeed, he had barely blinked, through all of the long hours that the flight had taken. The young wolf guessed that he had been brought a long, long way from the Forest of Tolokovin and, therefore, that he could not expect the wolf-pack to come to his aid. What was more disturbing, there had been no sign of Count Alucard throughout the flight – Skopka had begun to wonder if the Transylvanian nobleman had also been left a long, long way behind. Skopka need not have worried.

Although he had been sleeping soundly, and despite the fact that the landing had been perfect, the vampire-bat was wide-awake the moment the helicopter's wheels touched down on the landing-pad. It was lucky for him that he was. The aircraft was illuminated in a circle of brilliant spotlights. As the rotor-blades came to a stop, several shadowy overalled figures emerged from the dark beyond the ring of light, and began to run towards the helicopter.

Blinded by the dazzling light, the vegetarian vampire-bat blinked as he unfolded his wings. He shivered as he realised how cold he was and guessed that he must have been in flight, hanging underneath the helicopter, for several hours. With difficulty, for he realised that he was suffering from cramp, he eased his claws, one by one, from off the metal bar. There was no time to lose. Disregarding his discomfort, the vampire spread his wings then, thrusting his furry body forward, launched himself into the night air and towards the welcoming dark which lay beyond the circle of light.

Flitting to and fro, the vegetarian vampire rose up over the heads of the several running figures as they approached the helicopter and without so much as glimpsing him. But even if they had caught sight of the small, dark creature zapping overhead, the newcomers would have paid the small bat scant attention. They had other matters on their minds.

"How did it go?" said the man who arrived first at the side of the helicopter.

"Mission accomplished!" Captain Roth called back as he slid open the hatch and gave the man a double thumbs-up sign.

"Take a look for yourself," cried Albert Hoffmeyer, jerking his head at the helicopter's hold, as the remaining men in overalls arrived on the scene. "But don't get *too* close," he added with a chuckle. "The wretched animal stinks worse than a barrel-load of skunks."

"Stink or no stink, that's a genuine Transylvanian wolf inside that cage," said Captain Roth, as he lowered himself to the ground. They're an endangered species and it cost a fortune in grobeks, I don't mind telling you." Then, as he set off across the landing-pad and towards a row of single storey buildings beyond the ring of lights, he called back over his shoulder. "Get it across and settled into a bigger cage as quickly as you can. Let's see how the flea-ridden wretch takes to life in captivity?"

"If it doesn't like it, it will have to lump it," muttered one of the men, to the others, with a shrug. "One thing's for certain: that it will stay here, God rest its soul, until the day it dies."

"Are you going to stand gossiping all night?" snapped Albert Hoffmeyer, to the cluster of men outside the helicopter. "Climb aboard and get the filthy animal out of here – I've had enough of it." Then, with a yawn, he added: "Besides, it's been a long night. I would like to feel my head rest on a pillow before the

43

dawn comes up."

"Let me go first," offered a late arrival, a burly man who was brandishing a stout stick. "If the ugly brute turns nasty, I'll give it a whack with this."

One by one, led by the armed latecomer, the men in overalls clambered up and into the helicopter's hold.

Inside the cage, blinking at the light that flooded in through the open hatchway, Skopka began to whimper once again and inched back as the men approached, until the bars at the back pressed hard through his fur and into his haunches.

"*Ah-WHOO-ooo-ooooh!*" Skopka's whimpering had turned into an urgent whine.

"Keep quiet, you wretch!" the man with the stick commanded. Then, to prove his point, brought it crashing down across the bars which formed the roof of the cage. "Quiet, I say – or next time you'll feel the weight of this across your hide!"

"*Ah-WHOO-ooo-ooooh!*"

Some hundred metres or so away, standing in the sheltering dark beyond the circle of light, Count Alucard, having turned back into his human form, listened to Skopka's whining with a sense of growing frustration. The vegetarian vampire would have dearly loved to have gone to the young wolf's assistance, but what would that have accomplished for him, when he was one man against so many – apart from revealing his presence to his enemies *and* getting himself captured?

"No," the Count murmured to himself. "The only advantage that I hold over them at this moment, is

44

that they do not know that I am here. Better to lie low, for the time being at least, and await my opportunity to mount Skopka's rescue."

As he spoke, the vegetarian vampire glanced over his shoulder and realised, partly to his surprise but mostly to his dismay, that the first rays of the sun were stealing over a distant mountain range. It would be light in minutes. He would need to find somewhere to hide – and quickly. Across at the floodlit helicopter the men in overalls were manhandling the iron-barred cage out of the aircraft's hold and out on to the landing-pad.

Count Alucard knew that the circle of spotlights, blazing inwards and into the faces of the men, formed a barrier past which they could not see. But once they moved outside that ring of light, and as morning approached, he himself would be clearly visible. On top of which, who was to say that there were not other folk around at that hour of the day? It was growing lighter by the minute and before very long, his presence would be plain for anyone to see.

As the dark of night turned to lighter grey, the Count's sharp eyes blinked nervously as he took in his surroundings. An outline of several single-storey buildings was gradually taking shape and, judging by their size, Count Alucard guessed that he had arrived at some sort of private airport. Luckily, there were no lights or any other signs of life at any of the buildings and he judged that, provided he kept himself out of sight of the gang of men, he would be safe, at least for the time being.

About fifty metres from where he stood, a small, brick-built store-shed was becoming visible. Over at the helicopter, the gang of men had hoisted the iron cage containing Skopka on to their shoulders and, bowed under its weight, were making slow but steady progress towards the rim of the circle of light and in his direction. Deciding that the store-shed's walls would afford him sufficient protection from prying eyes for the immediate moment, Count Alucard sprinted across on his long, thin legs and hid himself behind the building.

It was a good job that he did so. A bright golden segment of sun was now peering over the rim of the far-off mountain range, bathing the slopes below, spilling all across the countryside and creeping over the stretch of grassland that contained the little airport. Also, and more important, as the Count plucked up the courage to poke his head round a corner of the building, he saw that the group of men, puffing and panting, had drawn almost level with his hiding-place. Pulling his head back hastily, Count Alucard held his breath and waited until he judged that the men had moved on before daring to peer out again.

As the group trudged off, in the early light, with the cage chafing at their shoulders, the Count could make out the now silent and despondent Skopka lying full-length on the cage's floor. Lowering his gaze, he was also able now to read the wording which was printed across the back of each man's overall:

ZEELANDER'S PRIVATE ZOO

"So *that's* what this is all about!" Count Alucard muttered fiercely to himself, peering around the corner of the store-shed as the group moved onwards and away from him. "They've kidnapped Skopka. They've snatched him from Tolokovin Forest, where

46

he was born and which is his home, and they're planning to put him in a *zoo*!" The Count was fairly shaking with rage as he continued: "They'll put him, at best, inside a fence with half a dozen trees to mope in. Or worse still, inside a cage where he has barely room to move." Count Alucard paused. He was not normally given to anger, in fact, in spite of the fact that he was a vampire Count by birth (albeit a vegetarian one by nature), he could be considered among the gentlest of men. But the thought of what the kidnappers had got in store for the young wolf caused the Count to fairly seethe with fury. "Over my dead body!" he stormed to himself.

For the moment though, Count Alucard knew that he would need to dispel his anger. If he was going to rescue Skopka, he would have to stay calm and keep his wits about him. The best time to attempt a rescue, he told himself, would be after dark and not during daylight hours. And the best thing that he could do right now, would be to find a place where he could safely hide away all day. He could not turn himself into a vampire bat in daylight hours, and that ability, as past experience had proved on more than one occasion, was very useful when it came to outwitting his adversaries. Also, and this time it was his appetite that reminded him, he would need to get himself something to eat.

The Count watched as the group of zoo-keepers (as their overalls had now identified them), still carrying the captive animal, moved off between some airport buildings and out of sight. About a minute later, he heard the sound of a vehicle's engine starting up. Next, he heard the vehicle moving off but Count

Alucard was unconcerned about the young wolf being driven away. He knew that he would have no difficulty in finding Skopka again, as soon as it was necessary. He knew that Skopka was being taken to "Zeelander's Private Zoo". A zoo would not be a difficult place to track down.

Another thing that he would need to do, Count Alucard told himself, would be to find out where he was? All he knew was that he had travelled on a helicopter for most of the previous night, possibly refuelling while he had slept? He had not the slightest idea about his present whereabouts? But there were clues that hinted at his being a long, long way from Alucard Castle and the Forest of Tolokovin.

Count Alucard breathed in deeply – exhaled, and then breathed in again. He savoured the tang of salt air at the back of his throat and, if he listened carefully, he could hear the sound of waves lapping along a sanded shore. His vampire bat's keen senses of taste and hearing had told him that one thing was certain: he was close to the sea.

4

Roscoe Zeelander breakfasted slowly, savouring each pleasurable moment. Breaking a warm croissant into several pieces, he spread one of these with butter, heaped it with a teaspoonful of apricot jam, then popped it into his mouth. Having washed down the tasty morsel, first with a swig of freshly-squeezed orange juice and then a gulp of sweet, milky coffee, he leaned back in his chair and peered over the balcony of the terrace of his villa, at where a myriad sunbeams danced across the ripples on the sea. Roscoe Zeelander belched, loudly.

"Pardon!" said Roscoe Zeelander, across the table and at no-one in particular, for he was breakfasting alone. He belched again, this time without an apology, and then began to hum a little tune, drumming his podgy fingers on the glass-topped table. Roscoe Zeelander was a happy man that morning. "And why not?" he congratulated himself. Not only was he very rich, he also possessed everything that any man could possibly desire.

As he continued eating his breakfast, Roscoe Zeelander counted his blessings inside his head. He owned a grand villa by the sea; a private helicopter; a jet-plane; a motor-launch; several cars; any number of valuable paintings; a large quantity of very large diamonds which he kept in a safe in the bank and, what was more, he owned a private zoo.

Roscoe Zeelander pursed his lips and frowned. That last thought was not quite true. He didn't *really* own a zoo. He *almost* owned a zoo. He owned those kinds of constructions that every zoo contains: a monkey house; a penguin pool; a crocodile lake; a flamingo pond; an elephant paddock, two bear-pits (one for brown bears, one for polars) and a wide variety of other sorts of animal runs and cages. He also employed a number of zoo-keepers, who had "Zeelander's Zoo" stamped across the backs of their overalls, and whose living-quarters were ranged alongside those buildings which, in the fullness of time, would resound with the howls, hoots, barks, whoops and urgent chatterings of all kinds of birds and animals.

And there, in those words "the fullness of time", you have the nub of Roscoe Zeelander's predicament. For while he was in possession of the cages, pits and fenced areas that make up the skeleton of any zoo, what Roscoe Zeelander's zoo lacked was inhabitants. So far, the zoo contained two exhibits only: a parrot, that had arrived two weeks before, and a Transylvanian wolf, that had arrived during the previous night and which the zoo's owner had not yet set eyes upon.

The reasons for this shortage of animals are easily explained. Firstly, the zoo's contruction had only been completed a couple of weeks before and, secondly and most important, the specimens with which Roscoe Zeelander sought to stock his zoo were all to come from endangered species. For that reason, they would have to be kidnapped from their natural habitats by unscrupulous hunters, rather than purchased through the usual channels. Kidnapping takes time. Roscoe Zeelander was a very rich man, but the one thing that money cannot buy is "time".

The millionaire was also an impatient man. He hated having to wait for things. More than anything in the world, Roscoe Zeelander wanted to see his zoo packed to its iron-barred cages and steel-meshed pens with birds and animals. But, rich as he was, there was nothing that he could do to speed up the arrival of the zoo's exhibits.

Roscoe Zeelander frowned again as he munched on his second croissant of the morning and, at the same time, turned his thoughts to the parrot. Peppina had been a big disappointment. Fetched from her home in a South American rain forest, Peppina was not young. She was slightly balding and was missing several tail-feathers. And, although Roscoe Zeelander had been promised a "talking" bird by his suppliers, Peppina had not uttered a single word from the moment she had arrived at Zeelander's Zoo. She had not even let out a single "squawk". Except for those few moments when she shuffled back and forth uneasily on the perch which stretched across her cage, Peppina sel-dom moved, contenting herself with sitting hunched, her head sunk deep in her shoulders, staring moodily out through the wire-mesh at the empty world of the zoo beyond.

Having begun his breakfast cheerily, a few short minutes before, Roscoe Zeelander was surprised at finding himself in a mood which seemed to match the same sombre outlook as the parrot's. For a moment, the millionaire wondered if the ailment the bird was suffering from might be catching?

"Pull yourself together, Roscoe!" the zoo owner told himself, dipping a silver teaspoon into the fine porcelain preserve-pot, then heaping apricot jam across a sizeable chunk of his second croissant. He was pleased, at least, to realise that his ill-humour had not affected his appetite.

Reaching out a stubby forefinger Roscoe Zeelander pressed a bell-button on the table. Seconds later, a manservant, wearing a white linen jacket with gold buttons, black trousers, and sporting a huge, drooping black moustache, came out on to the wide, white-tiled terrace.

"Ring down to the gate-house, Omar," the millionaire advised his manservant. "Tell them to have a limousine waiting for me, outside the front door, in half an hour."

"Yes, master," replied Omar, with a little bow. He was a well-built man whose thick upper-arms bulged through his jacket sleeves, while his calf muscles showed tight through his trouser legs. As well as being a manservant, Omar was also Roscoe Zeelander's bodyguard.

Roscoe Zeelander reached out a hand and felt underneath the crisply-ironed white linen napkin which was spread over the wickerwork croissant basket to keep the contents warm. Not that the napkin was needed any longer. The sun was now fully risen over the distant range of mountains, bathing the terrace with its warmth and melting the butter in the butter-pot.

As protection against the strong rays of the sun, Roscoe Zeelander pulled up the hood of his fluffy white dressing gown and drew it over his shiny bald head. He rubbed the thumb and fingers of one hand across the short, black stubble on his chin. Just one croissant more, he told himself, spread with the melting butter and heaped with the delicious apricot jam, then he would shave, shower and dress, and then have his chauffeur drive him round to the zoo where he would inspect the new arrival: the Transylvanian wolf.

Count Alucard glanced upwards, above his head, at where the sunlight filtered through the network of leafy branches, then drew back further inside the little grove, to seek what shade he could from the growing heat of morning, and also to hide himself from any prying eyes. Having left the airport as the sun came up, the vegetarian vampire had set off across the surrounding open countryside, striding out as fast as his spindly legs could carry him. It was important, he had told himself, to find a hiding-place before the day grew very much older. Still unaware of his exact whereabouts, the Count had guessed that his mode of dress: black jacket and trousers, stiff white shirt and neatly knotted bow tie, would be sure to draw attention to himself, were he to cross the path of any local inhabitants.

After having walked for half an hour, or thereabouts, and thankfully without coming across a single soul, he had chanced upon the little grove of orange trees. It was not, he had to admit to himself, the best of hiding-places, but it was the only one on offer, and so he would have to make the best of it.

Settling himself down on the sanded ground, Count Alucard eased his back against one of the trees and then spread his long legs out in front of him. He considered his situation. The orange grove was no more than thirty metres across in any direction but, provided no one came that way, he would be safe enough. Also, on the credit side, the trees were heavy with fruit. He would be able to quench his thirst on orange juice, while the flesh of the orange would more than satisfy his hunger.

For a second time, Count Alucard glanced upward. Judging by the sun's position in the sky, it was not yet mid-morning. Reaching inside his jacket, he pulled that month's issue of *The Coffin-Maker's Journal* from out of his pocket. He had put it there the day before for safe keeping. Settling himself as comfortably as possible, the vegetarian vampire flicked through the pages of his favourite magazine, looking at the coloured illustrations of the different kinds of coffins. Raising a hand, his long, slim fingers closed round a plump, firm orange and, pulling downwards, he plucked it from its branch.

Count Alucard bit into the orange with his two front pointy teeth. The juice spurted between his lips and his bat's keen sense of taste revelled in the sweetness.

He would have a long wait until nightfall, but he intended to make his stay in the orange grove as pleasant as was possible. Then, when darkness finally arrived, the Transylvanian nobleman would set off, locate Zeelander's Zoo and, by hook or by crook, contrive Skopka's escape from his prison.

Count Alucard had no doubts at all about his ability

to complete this self-appointed task, but as to how he and Skopka would return to far-off Transylvania, and the Forest of Tolokovin, when the escape was over, was a vexing question he would have to face up to when that time arrived.

"It's not as big as I expected, Anton," said Roscoe Zeelander, frowning as he peered into the cage which the head zoo-keeper had chosen for the new arrival.

"He'll grow," replied Anton Slivowitz, with a shrug, adding: "He's not much more than a cub."

"And why is it cowering at the back of the cage?" the zoo's owner enquired, crossly. Roscoe Zeelander was a very wealthy man but, like most rich men, he did not like to think that his money was being wasted. The millionaire frowned as he considered how much had been laid out already on his zoo exhibits – and what did he have to show for what he had spent? A bald-headed parrot that didn't talk and a cowardly runt of a mangy wolf. "Why doesn't it come down to the front of the cage and growl or snap its jaws or something?"

"If you like, Mr Zeelander," suggested the head keeper, "I'll get a couple of men to fetch broom handles and give it a good poke – that would make it stir itself."

"Not now," snapped the millionaire with a shake of his head. "But before I come back, in a week from now, I'd be grateful if you'd get it to behave like a *real* wild animal. Teach it to bare its teeth and frighten folk, instead of sitting there whining and whinging in the shadows."

"Very good, Mr Zeelander," replied Anton Slivowitz, touching his cap at his employer.

A moment later, Roscoe Zeelander had gone, with Omar, his bodyguard, in close attendance. Anton Slivowitz, who had other matters to attend to, walked away from Skopka's cage without giving the occupant another glance. He had a whole week in which to teach the wolf new tricks and the first painful lesson could wait for a day or two.

Left alone, the young wolf did not move. The truth of the matter was that he had paid scant attention to the men who had been peering in at him. Skopka's world, at that moment, consisted only of the space within the walls and bars that surrounded him, and what went on beyond that area was of no interest to him.

Skopka considered his situation. Admittedly, he told himself, he had more room now to move in than he had been afforded in the iron-barred box in which he had spent the previous day and night. But not *that* much more. There were four wolf's paces along the back wall of his present cage; and three wolf's paces from the back wall to the bars at the front. He had padded out those distances, his tail between his legs, a score of times and more that morning. Why not? He had nothing else to occupy his time. Skopka's canny animal sense told him that the space in which he was now enclosed was intended to contain him for a long, long time to come.

Unless, of course, someone should come along and rescue him? The young wolf still clung, desperately, to the few words of encouragement which had been whispered at him in the dark by Count Alucard, the night before. There had been neither sight nor sound, nor even a whiff of the Count's scent from that time to this, and Skopka's hopes were fading.

Settling himself down, full-length, with his belly pressed flat against the concrete floor and with his nose laid between his outstretched front paws, Skopka began a long, low self-pitying whimper:

"Ah-wher-wher-wher-wher," he went, but the whimper ended not long after it had started, as a strange, shrill voice spoke, seemingly out of nowhere.

"Buenos dias, amigo!" said the voice.

Skopka did not understand the meaning of the words, he was not even aware that he had been spoken to in Spanish, but he did seem to detect a friendliness in the chirpy tones. He pricked up his ears, lifted his head slightly, and peered out through the bars of his cage. There was no-one there. Outside his cage, the patch was empty. He was all alone.

"Buenos dias, amigo!" the voice said again. If Skopka had been born in Spain, he would have know that someone was saying "Good-day" to him.

Locating the origin of the sound at last, Skopka's pricked ears drew his eyes in the direction from which the words had come. Looking through the bars at the left-hand side of his cage, the young wolf found himself looking into the cage which stood immediately next to his own. At first glance, it seemed as if the next-door cage was empty.

"Buenos dias! Buenos dias! Buenos dias!" The same two words were squawked three times, almost angrily and in quick succession. They were accompanied by the sound of ruffling feathers.

Skopka's eyes moved upwards and he took in the cage's occupant who was perched on a wooden bar and was looking down at him. The strange bird was slightly larger (or so it seemed to Skopka) than the wood-pigeons which lived in the Forest of Tolokovin, and was more brightly coloured, being red and green and blue, and with a touch of yellow on both cheeks. As the parrot ruffled up its feathers for a second time, then dipped its beak, Skopka noticed that the bird had no plumage on the top of its head.

"*Sí, sí, señor!*" cried Peppina, the South American parrot.

For the first time, Skopka realised that it was the bird that had been making all the fuss – and not with birdlike "tweets", but words, as if it were a human being. Skopka, hardly able to believe his pricked-up ears, cocked his head first on one side, then the other, and stared at the parrot, mouth open, tongue lolling, in amazement.

At the same time, Peppina took three short steps along her perch, three steps back, cocked her head from right to left, and stared back at the Transylvanian wolf. The parrot, who had not previously uttered a word since the day she had left her native South America, had found her tongue again. Having recognised, in Skopka, a prisoner like herself, she was anxious to communicate with him.

"Buenos dias, amigo!" Peppina repeated perkily.

"Ah-wher-WHOOF!" went Skopka. The young wolf was still bemused at hearing a bird make human sounds, but animal instinct told him that he had found a friend.

"Buenos dias! Buenos dias! Buenos dias!"

"Ah-WHOOF! Ah-WHOOF! Ah-WHOOF!"

"Caramba!" screeched Peppina, joyfully.

Beneath a star-filled sky, the vampire bat skimmed low across the moonlit bay. It passed the little quay-side where a single motor-launch was moored, then rose upwards, on widespread wings, to fly over the sprawling villa where a lonely figure stood on the wide, white-tiled terrace, glass of wine in hand, looking upwards.

"A bat – that's unusual!" murmured Roscoe Zeelander to himself, as the black-winged, furry-bodied creature flew over his head, then flitted off, along the length of the terrace. "Aren't bats supposed to be endangered species? I wonder how you'd go about catching one?" The millionaire pondered to himself. But the vegetarian vampire bat was already out of sight and heading inland.

Fifteen minutes earlier, Count Alucard had been surprised at discovering how quickly the day had flown by. Sitting in the shade provided by the grove of orange trees, engrossed in the pages of *The Coffin-Maker's Journal,* and with as much of the sweet, juicy fruit as took his fancy a mere hand's reach away, the Count had glanced up to realise that the sun was dipping down behind the horizon. He had waited patiently until the first star of the evening was twinkling in the sky, before clambering to his feet, slipping his magazine back into his inside jacket pocket, then striding out from the shelter provided by the fruit trees, and into the open countryside. There was work to be done. Taking hold of the hem of his black, scarlet-lined cloak with both hands, the Count had spread his arms wide apart, taken a deep breath, then launched himself upwards, into the evening sky.

Leaving the villa behind him, cruising a couple of hundred metres high, the Count flew onwards. Almost immediately, Zeelander's Zoo came into view. Despite the fast-fading evening light, the zoo was instantly recognisable by the high wall which surrounded the widespread collection of single storey buildings and grassy fenced-in paddocks.

Gliding downwards, Count Alucard flitted over and across the zoo and was pleased to discover that the entire area appeared to be unguarded. There were some signs of life and lights switched on in one row of buildings, which he guessed, rightly, to be the zookeepers' living quarters. But apart from the occasional security floodlight, positioned at intervals about the walkways, there were no indications of any human presence – which surprised him slightly.

It was safe enough, the vegetarian vampire decided, to turn back into his human form. After hovering for several seconds on beating wing, about a metre and a half above the ground, the transformation took place and the Transylvanian nobleman's feet, encased in their black shiny shoes, touched down inside the zoo. Pausing only to straighten his white bow tie, which had somehow gone crooked during his change from bat to man, the Count set off along the nearest path, in search of Skopka.

It was only then that Count Alucard realised why there were no guards on patrol – there were no animals to be guarded! For, up until that moment, Count Alucard had not been aware of the lack of exhibits in Zeelander's Zoo.

"Good!" he exclaimed to himself. "All I need to do is locate the one cage that contains Skopka, give him back his freedom, then together we'll make our way out of this place, as speedily as possible, and without setting off any alarms." The most important thing, he told himself, was to proceed quietly and with caution – for while there were no guards on patrol, there were keepers aplenty in their quarters, and the slightest sound might bring them running out. In order not to make any noise at all, Count Alucard went on tiptoe.

"*Olé, señor!*" a voice screeched out as the Count turned a corner, then, for good measure, the parrot added: "*Caramba!*"

Count Alucard, startled, leaped in the air. Then, panicking at the thought of keepers arriving from all directions, he glanced all around in an attempt to spot where the unexpected voice had come from? It did not take him long to locate the source. First of all he spotted the printed sign above the cage:

"Peppina" – South American Parrot

Lowering his glance, the vegetarian vampire's eyes met those of the parrot. Still sitting on her perch, her head cocked to one side, Peppina stared Count Alucard straight in the face.

"*Buenos dias, amigo!*" squawked Peppina, lifting her left foot, then putting it back down and lifting up the right.

"Hush!" hissed Count Alucard, pressing a forefinger to his lips.

"Buenos dias! Buenos dias! Buenos dias!" Peppina, having regained her tongue through her new friendship with her next-cage neighbour, was eager now to strike up a conversation with anyone who chanced to pass by. Count Alucard was the first human to have done so.

But the Transylvanian nobleman, for the moment at least, chose to ignore the parrot. He had become aware of a soft, eager snuffling coming from the next cage along the row.

"Ah-wherrrrr." whimpered Skopka. Although overjoyed at having sniffed Count Alucard's scent on the still night air, the young wolf was aware of the need for caution. Next, catching sight of the Count hovering outside the parrot's cage, the wolf's whimper turned into a low, soft whine.

"Skopka! At last!" murmured Count Alucard, his eyes alighting on the young wolf who had padded to the front of the cage and was swaying, excitedly, at his approach.

"Buenos dias!" shrieked Peppina, angry at her visitor for having moved on. *"Peppina! Peppina! Peppina!"* In order to draw the attention back to herself, the balding parrot called out her own name.

"Grrrrrr." growled Skopka, softly but sternly in the parrot's direction.

Peppina stretched her neck, ruffled her feathers, and peered at Skopka, curiously. She waddled along the length of her perch, then waddled the same distance back, but without making a single sound. It was as if, somehow, Peppina understood that the wolf was warning her to keep her silence.

"Well done, Skopka!" said the Count, wondering at how the wolf had succeeded where he himself had failed.

There was no time now though, the vegetarian vampire told himself, to puzzle over such matters. The important thing was for himself and Skopka to get out of the zoo and as far away as possible, before anyone realised that the wolf had gone. And the first thing was to find a means of releasing Skopka from the cage. The Count discovered that this did not present a problem. A quick inspection of the door of the cage revealed that it did not have a lock. All that the Count had to do was to draw back the bolt. He did so. The door slid open at his touch.

Skopka bounded out excitedly in a single leap on to the ground. Tail wagging furiously, the young wolf nuzzled up against his friend and licked his long, slim fingers with an eager tongue.

"Come, Skopka," Count Alucard urged, rubbing at the thick fur underneath the young wolf's jowls. "The sooner you and I are out of here, the better it will be for both of us." Then, gesturing at the wolf to fall in at his side, the Count set off in a long, loping run, along the path between the cages which he hoped would lead him towards the zoo's exit. Moments later, he paused and looked back the way he had come.

Skopka had made no move to accompany the Count. Instead, the wolf had squatted on his hind legs, outside the parrot's cage, and was gazing, oddly, at the Count.

"*Skopka!* This way! *Quickly!*"

"*Grrrrrr.*" Skopka growled again, quietly, exactly as he had done a few moments before. Except that this time Skopka was not growling at Peppina – the young wolf was growling at his friend, the Count.

"Skopka!" snapped the Count, slapping his open palm against his thigh. "Come *on!* Now!"

Again the wolf made no show of moving. Instead, he turned his head, looked up into the parrot's cage and gave a little yelp: "*Ah-Wher!*"

"*Caramba, amigo!*" squawked Peppina, with a flutter of her wings.

In that same instant, Count Alucard realised what the problem was: Skopka was indicating that he wanted the Count to rescue the parrot as well as himself. As if he didn't have enough to worry about already!

Sneaking the wolf out through the gates of the zoo, past the keepers' living quarters, would prove difficult enough, but sneaking a wolf *and* a squawking parrot could prove one creature too many! Besides, the Count continued to himself, supposing he did succeed in freeing the bird, what would happen to Peppina once they had gained their freedom? Count Alucard guessed that the parrot had most probably spent too much time in captivity to be able to fend for herself in the big, wide world. And he certainly couldn't consider the bird's coming along with Skopka and himself, all the way back to Transylvania. What a thought! The very idea was preposterous.

"No, Skopka!" Count Alucard shook his head at the wolf. "We cannot take Peppina with us."

"*Grrrrrrr!*" Skopka growled more fiercely and the fur bristled along his back.

"No, Skopka!"

"GgggrrrrrrrrrRRRRRRRRR!" The young wolf's growl grew louder.

Peppina, meanwhile, had fallen silent. Sitting motionless, her balding head hunched between her shoulders, it was as if the parrot understood completely that her future lay in the balance.

Count Alucard walked back, slowly, to where Skopka stood, firmly, on the path outside the parrot's cage. After glancing down at the wolf, the Count looked in through the wire-mesh at the sad figure of Peppina whose bright eyes gazed back at him, solemnly and unblinking. A kind-hearted man by nature, Count Alucard suddenly felt a twinge of shame. A living creature, locked up in a cage, was in need of help and he had refused to give it.

"Oh, very well, Skopka," the Count said, with a weary smile. "All right, you win. The parrot shall come with us."

"Ah-WHER," went Skopka, approvingly.

"Olé! Olé!" screeched Peppina, twitching her tail and doing a sort of little jig.

"But only if both of you give me your solemn promise that neither of you will make another sound until we're safely away from this place." The immediate silence, both from the parrot and the wolf, was an indication that they would do as they had been told.

Peppina's release was effected just as easily as Skopka's freedom had been delivered. The Count pushed the catch at the side of the cage and the door swung open.

"Out you come, Peppina," said the Count.

The balding bird needed no second bidding. In two

66

hops and a clumsy flutter, Peppina had crossed the cage and, scenting freedom, her claws gripped the metal threshold underneath the open doorway. Then, letting out the softest of squawks, Peppina launched herself into the darkening night and in ungainly fashion (for she was unused to proper flight) about Count Alucard's head.

The vegetarian vampire and Skopka the Transylvanian wolf both glanced upwards at where the blue-green bird was shedding several small, fluffy feathers in her efforts at re-mastering the art of flying. She did not have much time in which to learn.

"We must be on our way, my friends," Count Alucard murmured, and the oddly-matched trio: man, animal and bird, set off along the pathway, in search of an exit. Count Alucard sprinted on his long, spindly legs; Skopka loped easily at his side, while Peppina, the South American parrot, discovered again the joys of free-flying as her beating wings kept her at a steady half-metre above the vegetarian vampire's head.

They moved in silence. The Count's shiny black pointed shoes trod lightly, while Skopka's paws barely seemed to touch the ground and the parrot's wings made not a sound.

In fact, there was not a thing to be heard throughout the zoo until the alarm siren rang out, crystal clear and deafeningly loud.

5

"A-WhoooooooOOOP-a-WhoooooooOOOP-a-Whooooooo-OOOP . . ."

The siren's wail rose and fell, splitting the calm of the night. Count Alucard, who had inadvertently set off the alarm, froze with sudden fear. Skopka, also terrified by the sudden clamour, cowered between the Count's legs while Peppina, equally afraid, fluttered down and sought the comfort of the vegetarian vampire's shoulder, nestling her downy cheek against his neck.

Count Alucard hugged the shadows just inside the entrance porch and held his breath while Skopka and Peppina, following his lead, were as still and silent as moonlit gravestones.

Their escape bid along the zoo's walkways could not have gone any easier. They had found the small, green-painted door which led to the outside world, and freedom, without the slightest difficulty. Better still, the door wasn't locked. It opened at Count Alucard's touch. But the alarm which was set to warn the zoo-keepers of any intruders that might attempt to enter the zoo, was equally efficient at warning them of the three would-be escapees seeking to get out.

"*A-WhoooooooOOOP-a-WhoooooooOOOP-a-WhoooooooOOOP!*"

Accompanying the siren, there were the sounds of instant activity from within the zoo-keepers' quarters which were situated just beyond the wall, followed almost immediately by the opening of a door and then the clatter of booted feet. As the Count, Skopka and Peppina huddled even closer into the shelter afforded them by the porch's shadows, a mass of keepers, some brandishing broomsticks, others wielding whips, barged in through the door by which the escaping trio had attempted to make their exit. Luckily, the keepers did not so much as glance into the nearby shadows. They reckoned the person, or persons, who had triggered the alarm must still be somewhere well inside the premises.

"You four search the left-hand path," cried Anton Slivowitz, pointing his head-keeper's silver-topped cane of office at one group of keepers. "And you four take the right!" he barked at a second lot. Then, beckoning at the ones that were left, he continued: "The rest of you, come with me – we'll take the middle route!"

Splitting up, the keepers set off along the paths as they had been directed. Count Alucard waited until the keepers' footsteps, and their voices, had faded off into the night before letting out a thankful sigh and venturing from the shadows. He turned his head, smiled reassuringly at Peppina still nestling on his shoulder, then stooped and gave Skopka an encouraging pat.

"Time for us to be on our way, my friends," he murmured as he stepped out, through the green door, and into the freedom of the world that lay beyond.

It was a warm, clear night. By now, the moon had risen to guide the trio on their way and the dark sky was sprinkled with stars.

With Skopka padding softly at his side, and Peppina fluttering above his head, Count Alucard stepped out in easy and unhurried strides, along the straight and narrow road which led, the oncoming salt breeze told his nose, towards the sea. There was not a soul in sight. Nor were there any signs of human habitation. If anyone should chance along, the Count had assured himself, he and his friends would have time to hide in the undergrowth which lay beyond the stunted trees on either side of the road. They could, of course, have travelled at a faster speed. But while the coast was clear Count Alucard had decided they would be best suited by moving at a leisurely pace and saving their energies, in case they had need to call upon them later. It was just as well that the Count had chosen so to do.

For although their moonlit stroll along the country road was a pleasant experience which did not present them with any problems, they had difficulties enough to face an hour or so later, when they approached the long, dark, sprawling villa and their fortunes took a turn for the worse.

"Someone's coming along the road!" hissed Omar. The big-biceped bodyguard was keeping watch on the moonlit road through a pair of high-powered binoculars, and had spotted Count Alucard approaching. "It's the animal-napper all right!" he added excitedly, as he swivelled the binoculars to take in Skopka, who was still padding patiently at the vegetarian vampire's side.

"Give those to me," growled Roscoe Zeelander, snatching the binoculars from out of his employee's hands and peering through them into the darkness. "The parrot's there as well!" he cried, spotting Peppina who was fluttering over the Count's head.

The Count was not to know that the dark block of buildings which they were now approaching was the home of Roscoe Zeelander, the millionaire zoo-owner. Neither was the Count aware that, having discovered their absence, head-keeper Slivowitz had already telephoned his employer and informed him that both his prized exhibits had been stolen.

Although he had no idea of the identity of the person, or persons, who had dared to break into his zoo, Roscoe Zeelander had taken matters into his own hands, and made preparations to capture the thieves, should they chance to come in his direction. As the Transylvanian nobleman and his two companions ambled along the road which ran alongside the villa, Roscoe Zeelander put his plan into action.

"Go! Go! Go!" yelled the zoo-owner.

In that same instant, the villa's security lighting was switched on.

Count Alucard, Skopka, and Peppina the parrot, found themselves blinking in the brilliance of the floodlights beaming down from high up on the villa's walls. Standing on the terrace, peering into the road below, Roscoe Zeelander was surprised to discover that the wrongdoer, standing as if transfixed by the light, was a tall, slim, pale-faced man with pointy teeth, red-rimmed eyes, dressed in a formal black suit, wearing a white bow tie and with a scarlet-lined black cloak thrown over his shoulders.

But there was no time now, the rich zoo-owner told himself, to ponder upon the thief's identity, or wonder about his curious choice of clothing. The most important thing at that immediate moment, was to arrest the villain and to regain possession of his stolen exhibits, then see them safely back inside their cages. Taking a silver whistle from his pocket, Roscoe Zeelander placed it between his lips and gave three sharp blasts. This was the pre-arranged signal for the front doors of the villa to swing open, and for some half-dozen burly servants to come rushing out into the road then bear down on the Transylvanian nobleman and his two companions who were still trembling in the glare of the security spotlights.

Luckily however, the whistle's blasts served, also, to jerk Count Alucard out of his stupor.

"Skopka! Peppina!" urged the Count, beckoning at both of his companions with a sweeping gesture. "This way!" Then, turning on the heels of his shiny black shoes, the vegetarian vampire set off on his long legs, with Skopka loping at his side and Peppina fluttering awkwardly overhead, back in the direction from whence they had first come. But if the Count believed that escape lay that way, his hopes were quickly dashed. Down that road, the three escapees were soon aware of lights approaching from the zoo's direction, accompanied by the sound of raised voices.

Having searched the zoo, and found it empty, the zoo-keepers, led by Anton Slivowitz, had snatched up lanterns and set off along the road towards their employer's villa, and the sea, in search of the missing zoo exhibits – and the rascal who had made off with them.

With the zoo-keepers, armed and angry, approaching them along the road, and the villa's servants, equally irate and coming towards them from the opposite direction, the three fugitives paused again on the floodlit road and pondered their plight. Count Alucard, had he so wished, could have turned himself into a furry creature of the night, sprouted wings, and found freedom in the night-sky. Peppina too, had she so desired, could have flown off in an instant. Such an idea did not occur to either one of them. There was no way that Count Alucard would leave Skopka to face capture alone; while Peppina, after spending so much time in lonely captivity, had no intention of deserting her two new-found friends.

For several seconds then, Count Alucard stood, shaking slightly and breathing hard, in the floodlit road. Skopka stood firm, close to the Count, the fur bristling all along the ridge of his back, teeth bared and growling softly, while Peppina hovered just above the vegetarian vampire's head, letting out one defiant screech after another.

"Now we have them, Omar!" murmured Roscoe Zeelander, smirking as he watched the events unfold from the safety of the villa's terrace. As his keepers approached along the road, the rich zoo-owner was able to see that some of them were carrying stout rope nets, while others had coils of rope slung over their shoulders. In the opposite direction the villa's servants had halted, spread themselves across the road, and were awaiting the arrival of the oncoming reinforcements from the zoo.

As if the combined army of servants and zoo-attendants was still not enough in number to overpower the quivering Count and his two companions, the approaching sound of whirring rotors warned the trio that still more of the zoo-owner's forces were closing in on them. Captain Roth, seated at the helicopter's controls and with the bespectacled, black-bearded Hoffmeyer beside him, hovered overhead.

The twin spotlights under the aircraft's hull added even more light to the scene below.

An urgent phone call from the villa a short while before had summoned the helicopter's crew to duty, from out of the comfort of their bunks. Cruising the area in search of the stolen zoo creatures, it had been the keen-eyed Captain Roth who had spotted the lights turned on outside the villa and had pointed the aircraft's nose in that direction, in order to investigate.

"There they are, Captain!" cried Hoffmeyer excitedly over the roar of the helicopter's engines, leaning out of the open door to blink down, through his glasses, at the activity in the road below. "They've got the wolf surrounded – I knew that ugly brute spelled trouble the moment that we took delivery of it from those peasant rogues in that forest."

"What else can you see?" asked Captain Roth.

"The parrot's there as well! And there's a tall, thin, funny-looking fellow, all togged up in white-tie and tails, as if he's going to a dinner-dance."

"White-tie and tails, Albert?" Captain Roth repeated scornfully. "I think it's time you got yourself some new glasses. Hang on! I'm going to take us down – we need to get a closer look at exactly what is happening."

With which, Roth eased back the controls and the helicopter banked, steeply, causing the navigator to hold tight, gulp twice, and then snatch at his breath.

In the road below, at ground level, the zoo-keepers, with ropes and nets at the ready, moved closer to the Count and his companions, while the servants from the villa slowly approached them from the opposite direction. The villa's long high walls, stretching along one side of the road, prevented escape in that direction, whilst the sound of the sea lapping gently against the harbour wall on the other side of the road warned the vegetarian vampire that there was no escape in that direction either. The three friends were cut off on all four sides, or so it seemed, and there was nothing to be done except wait and be taken prisoner.

Count Alucard's slim shoulders drooped. He sighed, and then sighed again. Skopka and Peppina would be returned to their cages while he could only wonder at what sort of fate was in store for him.

There was a brief pause, however, in the advancing ranks of men as the helicopter's engines suddenly grew louder while the down-draft from its whirring blades caused a wind which forced them to hunch their shoulders and hide their heads and, at the same time, whipped up a minor dust-cloud in the road. At the same time, as the aircraft banked again, the spot-lights underneath its hull picked out a rickety wooden jetty, on the harbour-side of the road, stretching out into the darkness of the sea. Count Alucard was quick to spot a possible escape route.

"Hurrah! There's hope left yet!" the Transylvanian nobleman murmured, as his right hand went down and gave the young wolf a reassuring pat, while at the same time he glanced upwards and gave Peppina an encouraging nod. "Follow me!" he added.

Then, in the shelter of the dust-cloud, with Skopka bounding at his side and Peppina fluttering at shoulder level, Count Alucard set off across the road and along the wooden jetty. The Count sprinted so lightly on his gangly legs that his black shiny shoes skimmed almost soundlessly along the wooden planking.

By the time that the helicopter had regained suffi-cient height for the dust-cloud to have settled, and the two groups of pursuers had cleared their throats and rubbed their eyes, they were surprised to discover that their quarry had vanished, seemingly into thin air.

"The jetty!" wailed the zoo-owner, shuddering with rage as he glared down from the terrace. "The rascal's taken my wolf and my parrot out on to the jetty!" Then, shaking his fists above his head, he added: "Get after them – before the villain takes my boat as well!"

As the words came out of Roscoe Zeelander's mouth, and as his servants and his keepers jostled against one another while they each strove to be first on to the narrow jetty, the sound of a boat's engine starting up out in the darkness told the zoo-owner that his precious craft was already in the enemy's hands.

"Don't stand there goggle-eyed, Omar!" snarled Zeelander, rounding on the bodyguard who was hovering at his shoulder. "Get on the radio at once and tell the helicopter crew to keep that boat in sight!"

Then, as the burly bodyguard strode off to carry out this last instruction, Roscoe Zeelander turned again and gazed out into the darkness, desparingly. The sound of the launch's receding engine advised him that his boat was already headed out into the dark of night and the open sea.

6

Standing in the boat's aft cockpit, feet apart and firm on the deck, Count Alucard turned the wheel and pointed the prow towards the darkening sea which lay ahead. Peppina had swooped down to settle on the Count's right shoulder and was blinking calmly, as she peered out at the twinkling stars. Skopka, on the other hand, had never come across the sea before and, nervous at the swaying motion beneath his paws, whined softly and sought reassurance by pressing his right flank against Count Alucard's left leg.

Although, truthfully, there was nothing that the young wolf need fear. Count Alucard knew how to handle a small sea-going craft.

When the Count had been a boy, his late father had often looked for privacy from the cares of the world by hiring a boat and taking himself, and his son, out into the silence of the vast Tolokovin Lake, for several days on end. During those times, the young Alucard had often had to handle the craft himself, while his father, a moody man by nature, had passed the hours by sitting on the foredeck and gazing pensively across the murky waters. But Count Alucard had never forgotten the sailing skills which he had learned as a boy.

Minutes before, when the Count had skipped along

the narrow jetty, with his two companions close behind, he had heaved a huge sigh of relief at seeing a boat so similar to the ones that he had handled all those years before, berthed in the murky shadows. After hastily unfastening the rope which secured the motor-launch to the jetty, Count Alucard had leaped down lightly on to the craft's aft cockpit.

"Here, Peppina! Jump, Skopka!" Count Alucard had urged, looking up towards the jetty from the well of the boat.

The bald-headed Peppina, who had just discovered that there was a comfortable perching-place to be enjoyed on top of Skopka's head and snug between his ears, had abandoned this resting-place at the Count's bidding and had fluttered down immediately to join him on the boat. Skopka, however, poised on the jetty's planking and peering nervously down, had seemed less eager to become a member of Count Alucard's crew.

Glancing back towards the entrance to the jetty, the vegetarian vampire had heard the growing murmur of raised voices, like a storm of angry bees, coming from the approaching men who were intent on making prisoners of himself and his companions.

"Jump, Skopka!" Count Alucard had repeated, then added "*Now!*"

It might have been the urgency in the Transylvanian nobleman's voice that had egged the young Tolokovin wolf into summoning sufficient courage to make the leap across and down on to the boat, or it might have been the fact that the craft was already beginning to drift away from the jetty. Perhaps it was a combination of both these reasons – either way, the wolf drew back on to his haunches, then launched himself into the air, across the widening black stretch of water, and landed squarely, on all four paws, alongside Count Alucard in the cockpit.

"Well done, Skopka!" the Count had exclaimed.

"*Sí, sí, señor!*" Peppina had squawked excitedly, then added: "*Caramba!*" With which, and at that moment, the parrot had fluttered up on to Count Alucard's shoulder.

With the pursuing forces left behind and seemingly helpless on the jetty, the Count took a firm grip on the wheel, with both of his hands, and concentrated all of his attention on the task in hand. His task, he told himself, was to steer his friends and himself as far away from the land as possible, and in the shortest possible time. For while he could not recall having seen any other boats moored alongside the jetty, he could not be sure that his pursuers did not have other craft nearby at their disposal. For all the vegetarian vampire knew, his enemies might be setting out from shore at that very moment – and in force. In which case, Count Alucard decided, it would be best if he were to keep his own lights switched off, at least until they were sufficiently far out to sea for them not to be glimpsed from the shore. The Count's hopes of escaping under the cover of darkness were quickly dashed.

The whirling roar of approaching rotor-blades warned the three fugitives that they were not yet out of danger. Less than a minute later, as the low-flying helicopter cruised across the calm waters, the motor-launch and its three occupants were suddenly bathed in the harsh glare from the spotlight fixed to the aircraft's underbelly.

80

"Si! Si! Si!" Peppina screeched, spreading wide her wings in fright but with her claws held fast as they gripped the shoulder of Count Alucard's cloak.

Ah-wher-wher-wherrrrrr" whimpered Skopka, dazzled by the spotlight's beam and with the fur along his back ruffled by the down-draft from the whirring blades.

"There, there, Peppina! Gently, Skopka!" The Count spoke soothingly to his companions and, at the same time, steered the boat in a zig-zag course, in an attempt to lose the helicopter cruising above the boat. But the motor-launch's throbbing, hard-worked engine was no match for the helicopter's fine-tuned and powerful rotor-blades. No matter how many times the small boat changed direction, the young male wolf, the bald-headed parrot and the vegetarian vampire remained transfixed in the blinding beam of light from directly overhead.

"Yes! *YES!*" cried Albert Hoffmeyer, shaking his clenched fists above his head in triumph as he peered down, blinking through his glasses, at the boat which was bobbing its way through the sea swell below. "We've got them this time, Captain," the navigator continued. "They can't escape us now. We can stay with them wherever they go. There are no hiding places out at sea."

"I'll take us down another ten metres," said Captain Roth, nodding in agreement and giving his navigator a double "thumb's-up" sign as he spoke.

"And I'll get on the radio and let them know, back at base, that we've got the missing exhibits, *and* the rogue that stole them, safely under surveillance," said

81

Hoffmeyer, rubbing his hands. "Mr Zeelander will be delighted when he hears the news. There'll probably be a reward in this for both of us."

"I wouldn't be too sure, Hoffmeyer," said Captain Roth, pursing his lips as he leaned forward and peered at the instrument panel. "And I wouldn't radio anyone, not for the moment, if I were you."

"Why not?"

"You wouldn't happen to remember, I don't suppose, the tasks I told you to perform this afternoon?"

The navigator put his head on one side and scratched his ginger beard as he thought hard for several seconds. "Of course I do," he said at last. "You asked me to do two things," he added.

"And what were they?"

"Well, first of all you said I was to wash up the coffee-mugs and tidy out the aircrew rest-room."

"And? After that?"

"After that you told me to make sure that there was plenty of fuel in the helicopter's tanks."

"And did you carry out those orders to the letter?" asked the helicopter pilot. "Think hard," he added.

"I remember cleaning out the rest-room and washing up the dirty coffee-mugs," replied the navigator, wrinkling his forehead as he turned his thoughts back to the events of that afternoon.

Captain Roth leaned forward, for a second time, and tapped at the fuel gauge on the control panel which was hovering near the "Empty" mark. "But you forgot to fill the fuel tanks?"

"I knew I'd forgotten something." The navigator gulped, swallowed, then gulped again. "My memory's getting worse and worse."

"I sometimes think, Hoffmeyer," Captain Roth began sternly, "that you'd forget to eat if your stomach didn't rumble to remind you when you're hungry."

"I'm sorry, Captain," said the navigator, deeply ashamed.

"There's no way that we can continue with the mission now," said Captain Roth with a shake of his head. "We've barely sufficient fuel to get back to base."

"What is there to say, except 'I'm sorry'?" Albert Hoffmeyer apologised for a second time as, far too embarrassed to look the pilot in the face he gazed down dolefully between his legs, drumming his feet on the aircraft's floor.

"It's no good saying 'sorry' to me," said Captain Roth, easing forward the controls and putting the helicopter into a steep turn. "Mr Zeelander's the person you will have to make your apologies to – and I shouldn't think that he'll be pleased. He's lost his South American parrot; he's lost his Transylvanian wolf, *and* he's lost his boat. I wouldn't care to be in your boots, Albert Hoffmeyer, when we get back to base."

The navigator made no reply. Taking a large, crumpled, grubby handkerchief from out of his flying-jacket pocket, he dabbed nervously at his brow. It was a cold night but Albert Hoffmeyer was not at all surprised to discover that his forehead was dripping with sweat. He was not looking forward to the meeting with his employer – not one little bit.

Count Alucard glanced backwards, over his shoulder, and watched the helicopter head off towards the mainland. The Count heaved a sigh of relief. He did not know why the helicopter's crew had chosen to give up the chase, but he was delighted by their decision. Once again, and thankfully, the boat was shrouded in darkness.

Minutes later, the moon came out from behind the low-lying bank of black cloud which had provided its hiding place for some time past. With the boat's throbbing engine taking the craft farther and farther out to sea, the Count glanced over his shoulder for a second time. In the pale light, he could just make out the coastline they had left behind them, but he and his companions, the vegetarian vampire assured himself, had sailed far enough from the shore to be out of sight themselves.

Sensing that the escape was complete, or very nearly, Count Alucard's spirits rose. So much so that he broke into a Transylvanian song which his father had sung to him when he had been a boy:

"Sovra zora,
Sovora dovra – dovrey,
Sovra zokra,
Sovola zokorato."

Taking his cue from his pointy-toothed, pale-faced companion, Skopka began to relax a little. The young wolf, although still a little nervous at the movement of the boat beneath his paws, was sufficiently confident, at least, to venture from the Count's side. Skopka took a couple of unsteady paces across the rear cockpit. Finding a coil of rope beneath a padded bench, the wolf nestled down comfortably and went to sleep.

Peppina meanwhile, unlike her four-legged companion, had no fears whatsoever in a calm sea.

Loosening the tight claw-hold she had been keeping on the Count's shoulder, she stretched her neck, ruffled her feathers and then stepped jauntily across his back to take up a new position on his other shoulder.

"*Buenas noches!*" squawked the South American bird, then: "*Buenas noches! Buenas noches!*" she repeated the words in quick succession.

"Goodnight, yourself," said Count Alucard who had travelled enough around the world to have picked up a smattering of Spanish and understood the parrot's words.

"*Olé!*" replied Peppina.

"The first thing that I shall do with you, madam, when opportunity presents itself," began the vegetarian vampire, keeping the boat on a steady course while turning his head until the end of his nose was touching the point of Peppina's beak, "will be to teach you to speak in a language to which I myself am more accustomed."

"*Caramba!*" squawked Peppina in the only language that she knew.

"You silly parrot!" said the vegetarian vampire losing patience. "Go to sleep."

"Go to sleep! Go to sleep! Go to sleep!" screeched Peppina, echoing Count Alucard's words in triplicate.

"Well done, Peppina!" cried Count Alucard, impressed at the bird's ability to pick up new words and phrases. Perhaps teaching the parrot to speak the same language as himself would not prove so difficult after all. "Say 'Count Alucard', Peppina, just for me? 'Count Alucard' – 'Count Alucard'?" The Count had tried to imitate Peppina's squawking tones.

Peppina was not listening. As if obeying the

86

Count's earlier instruction, the parrot nestled her bald head against the collar of Count Alucard's cloak and, following Skopka's example, fell fast asleep.

Count Alucard's eyebrows arched upwards in surprise. Not only was Peppina able to repeat his words she was also clever enough to understand their meaning. He had told her to go to sleep, and off to sleep she'd gone! But after a moment's thought, the Count smiled and shook his head. Wasn't it more likely, he told himself, that Peppina's eyelids had drooped with tiredness brought about by the adventures she had been through since her escape from the zoo? And also by the boat's gentle rocking motion?

"In fact," Count Alucard said aloud, blinking to keep himself awake, "I wouldn't say 'no' myself to a couple of hours sleep."

"Sleep! . . . Sleep! . . . Sleep!" Peppina repeated, squawking softly, shifting her claws' grip on the vegetarian vampire's shoulder and snuggling her body against the softness of his cloak.

Count Alucard glanced across the deck. Skopka, curled up on the coil of rope, was out to the world and snoring gently. The Count turned his attention to the moonlit waters which stretched as far as his eyes could see. It was the same on every side. Nothing but the softly lapping sea. The coastline, which was at his back, was long gone from sight. They were now far enough from land, Count Alucard decided, to be out of sight of prying eyes – certainly, there was not a sign of anyone coming in pursuit. It was safe, the Count decided, to switch on some lights.

Not long after, with the small craft fully illuminated and the ship's wheel set to hold the same steady course, Count Alucard set out to examine the boat from stern to stem. He did not pause for a moment to study the charts, the compass and other navigational instruments in the cockpit. What would have been the point? He didn't know how to use them. Having learned his sailing skills on Lake Tolokovin, he had never before sailed out of sight of land. Besides, he asked himself, what was the good of compass, charts and instruments, when he had not the faintest idea of where he wished to go? Count Alucard's concern, to put it at its simplest, was not in sailing off to somewhere else, but in sailing away from where he'd come.

Leaving the navigational aids behind, and with Peppina slumbering soundly on his shoulder, the Transylvanian vampire clambered, on his long legs, down the several steps of the short gangway that led from the boat's cockpit to take a peek at what lay below. He discovered that there were two identical small cabins, each of which contained a sleeping-bunk, a bunk-side table, a tiny wardrobe, a gleaming brass-ringed porthole, and little space for anything else. He also found a tiny cubicle, serving both cabins, inside which there was a lavatory, a shower and a wash-basin.

Count Alucard glanced only briefly at all of this accommodation, before turning his attention to that part of the boat he considered the most important: the kitchen – or, to give it its proper sea-going name, "the galley". For while the Count was of the opinion that he could sail away for several days without a care in the world and as free as fancy, he was well aware that he would need to give *some* thought as to what he, and his companions, were going to eat and drink.

Luckily, he soon discovered that both of the food cupboards in the ship-shape compact galley were well stocked with tinned goods. There were several stacks of tinned meats which, he was quite sure, would satisfy Skopka's needs, and a similar number of tins of fruit to suit himself. To his surprise, he was delighted to find a large jar of sunflower seeds, tucked away at the back of a cupboard – with the addition of an occasional morsel of fruit, Peppina's diet would present no problem. Most importantly, the Count was relieved to find that both of the boat's tanks of drinking-water were full to the brim.

"So far, so good!" the vegetarian vampire murmured to himself and then, "*Ouch!*" he added, as he banged his head on the galley's low door-frame.

"*Olé!*" squawked Peppina, drowsily, having been awakened by the sound of Count Alucard's forehead striking wood.

"I must remember to stoop in future when I move about below-decks," said the Count, gently rubbing his finger-ends against the tender spot on his forehead. Already, he felt sure, it was swelling into a bump. "This boat wasn't built for a gangly fellow such as myself."

"*Ah-wherrrrrrr!*" Skopka, having shifted in his sleep, on opening an eye and, finding himself alone, had clambered up on to all four paws and padded across the deck in search of company.

"Here, Skopka!" said the Count, glancing up at the young wolf who was standing at the top of the hatchway, wagging his tail and gazing down, eagerly, into the cabin's inviting light. "Come *on!*" Count Alucard urged, pointing at the short flight of steps which the wolf would need to negotiate. "Climb down, Skopka."

Skopka, however, had never before encountered a stairway. There were no flights of stairs in the Tolokovin Forest. In addition to which, the steps were rising and falling with the motion of the boat. Skopka whined again, softly, and drew back from the topmost rung.

"You can do it, Skopka!" the Count insisted, slapping the palms of his hands, encouragingly, against his thighs.

Skopka had a better idea. Drawing himself back on his haunches, the young wolf launched himself out over the hatchway. Skopka may not have been taught how to climb down a staircase, but he did not need lessons in how to jump.

The wolf's front paws struck Count Alucard squarely in the chest, sending him careening backwards. This sudden movement startled the dozing parrot on his shoulder. Peppina flew up into the air in a fluttering mass of feathers.

"*Caramba!*" screeched the South American parrot.

"*Ouch!*" cried Count Alucard collapsing on to the wooden floor and, this time, banging the back of his head.

Aghast at the damage he had caused and in an attempt to apologise for his misdeed, Skopka straddled the prostrate vampire's chest and slobbered a wet tongue energetically, all over the Count's pale face.

"Get off, Skopka!" wailed the Count, thrusting upwards with both his skinny hands in an attempt to shift the eager wolf. "I beg of you – get *off*!"

"Get off!" mimicked Peppina, still fluttering this way and that and, in her agitation, slapping her wings against the galley's low ceiling. "Get off! Get off! Get off!" she screeched.

"Hush, Peppina! Get *off*, Skopka!" With one last desperate shove, Count Alucard succeeded at last in pushing the enthusiastic wolf aside. Exhausted from his efforts, and with both the back and front of his head throbbing, the vegetarian vampire lay on his back for several moments, blinking through his red-rimmed eyes and gazing up at the galley's ceiling.

Skopka shook himself, licked his slavering chops, shook himself again, then cocked his head and fixed his eyes, enquiringly, on the recumbant Count. Taking her cue from Skopka, Peppina ceased her madcap fluttering and, perching on the brass rail which was positioned round the stove, lifted a wing and pecked inquisitively underneath her feathers as if nothing out of the ordinary had happened.

"Mercy on us!" gasped Count Alucard, hauling himself up from the floor and into a cross-legged position. Then, taking the white silk spotless handkerchief from out of his top pocket, he carefully wiped away the saliva, deposited by Skopka's tongue, from his face. "I rather think that we have had sufficient adventures to be going on with," the Count continued with a grimace as he slipped the soiled and sticky handkerchief back into his pocket, adding: "Go back to sleep."

"*Grrrrr!*" growled Skopka, lifting a back paw and scratching at a flea which had been lying doggo for several days in the thick fur beneath his neck, and which had suddenly decided to make its presence known.

"*Buenas noches!*" squawked Peppina.

"Follow me, my friends," Count Alucard said,

scrambling quickly to his feet. "I'll show you both to your cabin."

As the vegetarian vampire left the galley, Peppina fluttered after him instantly. Skopka stayed behind, long enough to take another two quick but unsuccessful strokes with the claws on his left back paw at the flea which had made its home in his fur. Then, giving up but still itching, the young wolf padded after his companions.

Count Alucard lay on top of the duvet which was spread across the first cabin's bunk. His copy of *The Coffin-Maker's Journal* lay open on the bunk-side table, where the vegetarian vampire had laid it down before settling himself for sleep.

The bunk was fastened to the side of the boat; the wardrobe was tight up against the foot of the bunk while the wooden partition, which divided the cabin from the rest of the boat, formed the bunk-head. Also, there was a strip of wood on the fourth side of the bunk, built to prevent the sleeper from falling out when the sea was rough. In short, the vegetarian vampire was enclosed, in the bunk, on all four sides. It was, the Count had been delighted to discover, almost like sleeping in a coffin – for which reason he slept soundly, flat on his back, feet together and with his arms neatly folded across his chest.

Peppina was perched atop the wardrobe in the second cabin, her head sunk between her shoulders, eyes shut tight. Skopka lay curled up on the bunk beneath, also fast asleep and undisturbed – the flea which had been causing problems earlier was sleeping too.

The boat lay still. The sea was calm. The sky was clear. The moon gazed down without so much as a single fleck of cloud to spoil its view. Even the moonbeams, that had shimmered merrily an hour or so before, were now lying motionless as if they too were sound asleep.

It was that kind of absolute calm that comes before a dreadful storm.

7

The rain came first. Lightly to begin with, and evenly, the raindrops showering across the sea's calm, moonlit surface and making barely a whisper. The light grey-coloured clouds proceeded at a leisurely pace, high up in the night sky. They passed over the now gently bobbing boat, allowing a host of drops to patter softly along the deck and pitter across the cabin's roof so quietly that neither Count Alucard, asleep below, nor either of his two companions, was aware of the oncoming dreadful weather.

Next came the wind. That too started gently. No more than a lively little breeze at first, heralding what was to follow, carrying the raindrops with it, encouraging them in a merry dance across the wooden deck and causing the boat to bob just a little higher than it had done before. But in the quiet of the cabins below, the Transylvanian vampire and his friends dreamed undisturbed, exhausted from their previous encounters and totally unaware of the nightmare adventure that was about to overtake them.

The rain clouds were bigger and blacker than before. They scudded in from the far horizon, picking up speed on the gusting wind. The rain began to fall heavily, also driven on by the wind, and whipped

94

across the surface of the sea which was, by now, rising and falling in angry fashion.

Both wind and rain grew worse. Below decks, as the boat keeled in the swelling sea, in the ship's galley and with no-one to watch its progress, the glass jar of sunflower seeds which the Count had neglected to put back in the cupboard, slid across the galley-table, teetered dangerously on the table's edge, then slid back the way it had come as the boat swayed in the reverse direction. Then, having arrived at the table's opposite edge, the jar teetered once again, before finally toppling over the edge.

"CRASH!"

"Saint Unfortunato preserve us! What was that?" Count Alucard cried, awakened instantly by the sound of the sunflower seed jar striking the floor and shattering into a thousand pieces. Sitting bolt upright, the Count blinked first, then gulped, as he digested the fact that the boat was at the mercy of a storm. The rain rattled on the cabin roof above his head. The wind howled as it raged all around outside the boat.

"*Ah-WHOOO-OOOooooh!*"

It was not the wind that had made that sound. Skopka, in the second cabin, was also awake and fearful of the storm. Lying on his bunk, the young wolf dug all of his claws into the mattress, through the duvet, and wished that he was somewhere else. He had known stormy nights in the Tolokovin Forest – but never anything to equal this ferocity!

"*Ah-WHOOO-oooOOOOH!*" the young wolf howled again.

"*Caramba! Caramba!*" screeched Peppina. The South American parrot had been awake for several minutes. Having abandoned her perch atop the wardrobe, Peppina fluttered her wings excitedly and attempted to hover in mid-air while the cabin tossed and pitched around her.

"*Caramba! Caramba!*" she screeched fearfully.

"I'm coming, Skopka! Keep calm, Peppina!" called Count Alucard, slipping a lanky leg over the side of the bunk and feeling tentatively for the shifting deck with his big toe. Keeping a tight grip with both of his hands on the wooden bunk-rail, he sent his other foot to join the one that had gone before.

The weather worsened second by second. Loosening his hold on the bunk-rail, the Count turned round slowly and, doing his best to stand upright, set off towards the second cabin. Two steps later he lost his balance. Staggering across the floor, he stumbled into the cabin wall, then lurched across, as the boat swung upwards, and bumped into the opposite wall with a painful thud.

"*Caramba!*" screeched Peppina from the other cabin.

"*Ah-whoo-OOO-oooh!*" whined Skopka, from the

same direction.

"I won't be long! I *am* coming! Don't be afraid!" Count Alucard called back at his friends, above the howling wind and rain.

Alas though, if truth be told, Count Alucard was far and away more frightened of the situation than either of his companions. The Count was not a brave man. He was very nearly (but not quite) a coward. Whenever danger threatened, the vegetarian vampire's first instinct was to run away and hide. Unfortunately, in his present position, there was nowhere he could go.

The boat was caught in a sudden massive sea swell which lifted it high up in the air, then dashed the vessel down again into the turbulent waters with a vicious slap. Thrown across the small space, the Count found himself back clutching at the bunk-rail from where he had started out.

Across in the second cabin, Skopka slithered, on all fours, across the polished floor. Having heard the Count's call, the frightened wolf had decided, foolishly, to attempt to join him. But Skopka's leap down from the bunk had proved too difficult a manoeuvre for his paws. Unable to gain a claw-hold on the polished floor, the wolf slid along the shiny planking and into the open wardrobe – just in time for the wardrobe door, which had been swinging to and fro in the gale, to slam shut behind him.

Peppina, meanwhile, had given up trying to stay airborne and immobile while the cabin pitched and swayed on her every side. Having flapped her way to the side of the cabin, the frightened parrot managed to clamp her claws around the brass fittings on the rim of the porthole. As the boat swung crazily, both from side to side and up and down, Peppina clung on to her claw-hold grimly, fluttering her wings to keep her balance and screeching with all her might.

"Skopka? Where's Skopka?" gasped Count Alucard as he staggered into the second cabin and was surprised at not finding the young wolf there. The Count clutched at the doorpost as he spoke, in order to stay on his feet.

"Skopka! Skopka!" Peppina echoed, wide-eyed and fearful of the boat's mad antics.

At that moment, the boat was snatched up on another giant wave which caused the wardrobe door to swing back open. Skopka, who had been huddled up inside the wardrobe and against the door, slid back out into the cabin, this time on his stomach and with his legs splayed out both in front of him and behind.

"*Ah-wher-wher-wher!*" whined the young wolf as, unable to control his progress across the shiny deck, he skidded past the Count and out into the galley where he ended up in a tangled mass beneath the galley-table.

One more enormous wave crashed against the side of the boat, this time bursting open the porthole and drenching Peppina before sending a shower of sea water all across the cabin floor.

"If this keeps up," the Count told himself, still struggling to stay on his feet, "we shall need to abandon ship before the vessel overturns and we are all three trapped beneath." But how, he asked himself, could he and his companions "abandon ship" when there did not appear to be a lifeboat with which to make their escape?

Fate offered a helping hand. Skopka had not had the wardrobe to himself. As the boat was lifted yet again – and yet again slammed down – a couple of life-jackets which had been tucked away on the wardrobe's top shelf, suddenly spilled out on to the cabin floor then, as the boat heaved in the other direction, slid across the shiny planking and came to rest at Count Alucard's feet.

"All is not lost!" the vegetarian vampire murmured, keeping one hand on the door-frame as he lowered himself, gingerly, snatched up one life-jacket then placed a neatly shod foot on the second, for fear that a sudden shifting by the boat might send it skidding out of his reach.

Putting on the first life-jacket, with one hand gripping the door-frame as the boat was tossed in all directions, was not an easy task. On board a boat in a raging gale and with sea water now spewing in from several directions, his mind was in a total spin. His fingers were all thumbs, while his thumbs paid no heed to his instructions. To make matters worse, Peppina, having suffered a drenching at the open porthole, had abandoned that position and, by careful use of claw and beak, had managed to negotiate a path round the cabin walls. As the Count fumbled, one-handed, with the life-jacket, Peppina fluttered about his face, trying to gain a perching place on top of his head.

"*Hola! Hola!*" screeched the parrot.

"Go away, Peppina!" urged the Count, brushing an elbow at the bird. Desist, madam! Get off me!"

But Peppina, having finally managed to wrap her claws around a lock of Count Alucard's long, black hair, did not mean to let go, and the more the Count tried to shift her, the more Peppina tightened her hold.

"*Oooh-er!*" the vegetarian vampire wailed as the parrot's grip tugged at the roots of his hair.

Despite the parrot's interference, the Count finally succeeded in getting both of his arms into the life-jacket. Then, judging the moment carefully, when the boat had been lifted up on the crest of a massive wave and hung perilously in mid-air, Count Alucard loosened his one-handed grip on the door-frame and tied the cords of the life-jacket faster than a life-jacket's cords had ever been tied before. Then, as the boat began to fall back down towards the turbulent sea, the Count grabbed back at the door-frame, stooped and snatched up the second life-jacket. He glanced across at where Skopka lay grimly curled around the leg of the galley-table, clamped securely to the deck.

Count Alucard let out a sigh. Putting on his own life-jacket had been hard enough, he told himself, but getting the second jacket on to Skopka was going to be a whole lot harder.

"Here goes!" the vegetarian vampire murmured, letting go of the door-frame as the boat keeled over, yet again, in the full force of the storm. With the second life-jacket tucked underneath an arm, and with Peppina's claws still entangled in his hair, the Count slid down across the tilted deck and, luckily, managed to grab hold of the table-leg opposite the table-leg which the wolf's legs were locked around.

"*Caramba!*" cried Peppina, with a flutter of her wings.

"Here, Skopka!" urged Count Alucard, with one arm wrapped around a table-leg, while holding out the life-jacket encouragingly with his free hand. "Let me get you into this."

As things turned out, putting the life-jacket on Skopka was not half so difficult a task as the Count had expected it would be. For although the young wolf had not the slightest idea of the purpose of the life-jacket, he seemed to understand that, in the Count's attempts to wrap the cumbersome object round his body, he had the wolf's best interests at heart. Even so, in order to achieve this end it was necessary for both Skopka and Count Alucard to release their hold on the galley-table. Then, while the boat continued to be tossed about by the storm, the pair rolled about the galley floor, as the vegetarian vampire struggled to secure the life-jacket around Skopka's middle.

By now, as the storm continued unabated, both the galley and the cabins were awash with sea water which was sweeping in, not only through the porthole but also gushing over the hatch at the top of the steps. Count Alucard and Skopka were both soaked to the skin. Peppina, at least, had the good sense at last to untangle her claws from the Count's long, black hair. Unsure of what was happening, the parrot fluttered about the galley, just above the slopping water, squawking persistently.

Thankfully, with patience and with perseverance, Count Alucard's task was finally completed. The second life-jacket had somehow been manipulated over the wolf's front legs and the cords tied securely over his belly. Out of breath but pleased with his achievement, the Count clambered to his feet. He was concerned to discover that the water level was rising and already over his trouser bottoms. He was equally worried that there was no indication of the storm blowing itself out.

"We must get up on deck, my friends – and as quickly as is possible," the Count advised his companions as the boat dipped into the trough of a wave and more sea water swept in over the hatch. "If this keeps up we shall be forced to abandon ship."

"Abandon ship! Abandon ship!" screeched Peppina, shaking her head as she repeated the Count's words, parrot-fashion.

"*Shush*, you tiresome bird!" chided the Count as he splashed his way, in two quick strides, across the galley to where the short steep flight of steps led up to the boat's aft cockpit and the outside deck. "Smartly does it!" he urged, gesturing at Skopka to go first. But if the young wolf had had difficulty earlier in coming down the steps, he would have far more trouble trying to get up them, hampered by the life-jacket tied round his middle and with the boat tossed frantically about in the wind and weather.

As Skopka lifted a trembling paw and gained a cautious foothold on the lowest step, Count Alucard speeded up the process by placing both of his hands behind the young wolf's haunches and giving him an almighty shove.

"Hop-la!" cried the vegetarian vampire and, Skopka scrambled clumsily up into the cockpit. Count Alucard picked up the parrot and placed her gently on his shoulder. "Off we go," he said and, taking a firm hold on both of the hand-rails, clambered up the steps as they rose and fell in the force of the gale underneath his feet.

102

If the weather had seemed rough to the three travellers while they had been below-decks, the conditions appeared to be twice as bad once they were up in the aft cockpit. The wind felt twice as harsh as it whipped across their faces. The boat itself was tossing all the more perilously. At one moment, the sea seemed to be thrashing turbulently below them, an instant later it appeared as if the same turbulent waves were pitching overhead to come crashing down on the gale-washed deck, in the black of night, in a mass of foamy spume and spray.

"Abandon ship! Abandon ship!" screeched Peppina, repeating again the last words she had learned, as she dug her claws into the Count's shoulder and cowered against the collar of his cloak.

"I sadly fear that you may be right, Peppina," Count Alucard murmured, as he strove to hold the ship's wheel but the sheer force of the gale sent it spinning round out of his hands.

Skopka, meanwhile, was huddled, frightened, on the floor of the cockpit. Up by the prow of the boat there was a small lifeboat which was secured, upside-down, to the deck, but under the present conditions there was no way that the Count would dare to venture out and attempt to launch the tiny craft. And even if he could find a means of getting the little lifeboat into the raging sea, how on earth was he going to succeed in coaxing Skopka out across the open deck, when he himself did not have the courage to put his nose outside the cockpit?

"But if we *don't* take to the lifeboat, we shall certainly perish when this boat sinks, as it surely must?" Count Alucard told himself with a shiver, as he struggled hard to keep his footing while the boat swung, first one way and then the other, in the raging sea.

If the sea was in a turmoil, so were the thoughts that turned and twisted inside the vegetarian vampire's head. Count Alucard did not know what to do for the best? If he had not had Skopka to consider, the Count would have made the change from man to flying creature. He could have taken wing and shepherded Peppina to safety, and beyond the wind and rain and, who knows, perhaps to some peaceful, distant shore? If, on the other hand, he stayed with the sinking boat and took his chances with the wolf, what would become of Peppina who, considering her age, could hardly be trusted to set out in search of land alone? Count Alucard was not a brave man, but he could not bring himself to desert Skopka – and yet, by staying with the wolf, surely he was condemning Peppina to a watery grave?

It was a vexing problem, and one which the Count would much rather not have had to consider at that particular moment. Luckily, if you care to call it luck, the problem was taken right out of Count Alucard's hands. For at that very moment, a gigantic wave, bigger by far than any that had gone before, took a firm hold of the boat, swung it upwards and above the rest of that swirling sea, then brought it crashing down on some hidden rocks.

"*Ah-whoo-OOO*—" the howl of fear from the panicking wolf was cut short before it had left Skopka's throat.

"Abandon—" began Peppina, but the second word never left the parrot's beak.

Count Alucard heard neither of these unfinished

cries. Nor did he hear the sound of splintering fibre-glass as the boat's hull came crashing down on the hidden reef, instantly splitting the craft cleanly in two across the middle. The vegetarian vampire had problems of his own at that immediate moment. Thrown across the cockpit by the force of the collision, the Count struck his head against the side of the boat and, as the craft keeled over on the razor-sharp rocks beneath, was blown off his feet by the buffeting wind and thrown into the stormy sea, where he immediately lost consciousness.

8

"Get off! Get away! Stop doing that!"

There can be nothing worse, after having lain unconscious, Count Alucard later told himself, than being brought back to one's senses by having a wolf's rough tongue slobber eagerly all across one's face.

"Cease, Skopka!" cried the Count. "Enough, I say! Desist this very instant!"

But the young wolf, delighted at discovering that his friend was not dead, but only stunned, licked all the harder and the warm saliva from the animal's jowls dripped over the vegetarian vampire's cheeks.

"Stop it! Stop it! Stop it!" wailed Count Alucard, scrambling up into a cross-legged sitting position. Then, taking his white silk handkerchief, soaked with sea water, from out of his jacket's top pocket, he wiped his face carefully. Although the sticky saliva was easily removed, the strong, tangy wolf-smell lingered on his cheeks, invading his nostrils. The Count sighed and pulled a face. The smell would stay there, he knew, until he found a means of scrubbing it away. The Count gave another sigh – a long one this time – then looked directly into the young wolf's face which was on a level with, and almost touching, his own.

"*Ah-wher?*" whined Skopka, enquiringly, his head

cocked on one side, his ears pricked, his tail wagging spasmodically, his eager eyes staring back at the Count.

"Thank you, Skopka – for returning me to the land of the living," said Count Alucard, relenting. After all, he told himself, if the wolf had not come along and licked his face, he would still have been unconscious. But what was this place, he wondered? And how had he come to be there?

The last thing the Count remembered, as he sat trying to collect his thoughts, was of being on board a sinking ship, on a stormy sea, in the black of night? But here he was now, on dry land, at early morning and without the slightest hint of bad weather? Raising his hands, the vegetarian vampire discovered that he was still wearing the life-jacket which he had donned the night before. A quick glance told him that Skopka was similarly clad. The life-jackets then had done their job and kept him and the young wolf afloat when the boat sank – but how had they both managed to make their way to land? An awful thought suddenly filled his head. There had been three of them on board that boat and now there were but two! What had happened to the third member of the party – the one that had not been blessed with a life-jacket? What awful fate had befallen Peppina?

"Buenos dias!" croaked the South American parrot, fluttering down from out of the sky and settling on Skopka's head. *"Buenos dias! Buenos dias!"*

"Good day to you too, Peppina," replied the Count, then: "All crew members present and correct," he murmured to himself thankfully, as he scrambled to his feet. The time had come, he told himself, to discover how he and his two companions had been saved from drowning?

He was standing, he discovered, on a sanded beach and with the sea lapping gently along the shore a couple of metres from his feet. It was not long after dawn and the sun was edging up over the far horizon. There was not a single cloud in the sky, nor was there a hint of any breeze. Without question, the foul weather was gone and a sunny day lay ahead. Still looking out to sea, with the light improving by the moment, the Count saw part of the boat's broken hull sticking up out of the water, not far from the shore-line.

"So that's what happened?" Count Alucard murmured to himself. They had been shipwrecked, mercifully close to land. Skopka and the Count, with the benefit of their life-jackets, had been thrown up on to the shore, while Peppina, despite the howling winds, would have had little difficulty in flying so short a distance.

After complimenting himself, and his friends, on their combined good fortune, Count Alucard turned his back on the sea and looked in the opposite direction. The fine golden sand on which he stood stretched back, smooth and unmarked, some fifty metres or thereabouts, as far as a stretch of patchy grass, beyond which there was a fringe of bushy undergrowth bordering a thickly wooded slope that rose up the side of a rock-strewn hill. Next, looking first to his left and then to his right, the Count saw that there were larger rocks on either side, which led across the sand and down into the sea – forming a bay into which the boat had foundered, driven by the wind, during the previous night.

"The first thing that needs to be done," the Count said, glancing down at Skopka who was fidgeting in the life-jacket, "is to get you out of that thing." With which, the vegetarian vampire stooped and fiddled with the knot he had hastily tied the night before.

Taking off the wolf's life-jacket was easier said than done. For there is nothing harder to unfasten than a clumsy knot which has not only been pulled tight, but is also soaking wet.

"Have *patience*, Skopka!" the Count commanded. But although there was nothing, at that moment, that the young wolf wanted more than to be rid of the encumbrance around his chest, his natural animal instincts forbade him from keeping still. The longer the Count's thumbs and fingers fumbled with the awkward knot, the more Skopka fidgeted and fretted. It was quite some time before Count Alucard succeeded in his task.

"There we are!" the Count exclaimed at last as he finally pulled off Skopka's life-jacket.

"*Ah-WHERRR!*" yelped Skopka in relief, and giving himself a good old shake.

"*Caramba!*" added Peppina, not wanting to be left out.

Having untied one life-jacket, Count Alucard turned his attention to the next, which was knotted around his own slim chest. This second knot proved easier to untangle than the first, mainly because the Count had the good sense to stand perfectly still while he attended to the task.

"And the next thing that needs to be done," Count Alucard said, as he tossed the second sodden life-jacket aside, "is to find a means of drying out these wet clothes I'm wearing." Then, turning his eyes towards the rim of the wooded hill, he added, "For if we are to set out, in that direction, in search of human help, it would be best if we were to present ourselves as neatly and as tidily as possible, and not dripping water from our coat cuffs or squelching wet inside our shoes with every footstep."

Shining down from out of a cloudless sky, the midmorning sun cast its warmth across the golden sand and over the rocks, while a host of sunbeams danced on the smooth waters in the bay where Count Alucard was taking a dip. The Count had put his life-jacket on again and was using it as a swimming-ring. He had never learned to swim. Sensibly though, on this occasion, he had tied the cords together loosely in a bow. There would be no problem when the time came for him to take the life-jacket off again.

Skopka was in the water too, but without the need of a life-jacket. Unlike the vegetarian vampire, the young wolf was a natural swimmer and had no fear of the sea – in daylight and in the calm waters of the bay. Peppina was pleased to join in the sport, but the parrot preferred to spread her wings and skim across the surface, squawking loudly as she went and sometimes flying so low that her feet trailed in the clear, blue water.

While the three companions exercised, Count Alucard's clothes which had been laid out neatly on a large, flat rock which jutted out into the sea, were drying in the sun. The Count's scarlet-lined black cloak; his frilly white shirt; his white bow tie; his black well-tailored formal jacket and matching trousers; his black silk socks; his white silk underpants which were tastefully embroidered on the bottom of one leg with the initials C.A.; his white silk handkerchief which normally peeped out of the top pocket of his jacket; his waterlogged black pointed shoes – all of these belongings were spread in two rows, most of them weighted down with pebbles, in case a breeze should chance to spring up and attempt to carry them away.

Another item on the rock, opened at the centre page and also weighted down with pebbles, was the Count's precious copy of that month's issue of *The Coffin-Maker's Journal*, which had been in his inside jacket pocket while he had been in the sea. He hoped that the magazine might be returned to a readable state from its present soggy condition.

"I do believe they're dry enough to wear!" Count Alucard announced about half an hour later, as he pulled on his silk underpants, having clambered up on to the rock to test the state of his clothing. A couple of minutes later he was fully dressed, with Skopka at his side and Peppina sitting comfortably on his right shoulder. "All ship-shape and in order!" the Count added, happily as he slipped *The Coffin-Maker's Journal*, which had dried off completely, back into his inside pocket.

Luckily, the vegetarian vampire did not have the benefit of a mirror in which to look at himself, or he might not have been in such good spirits. For, although the sun had dried out his clothing, every item he was wearing was badly wrinkled. Although, even if he had owned a mirror, it would not have served him any purpose – for vampires (as every student of the Dracula legend knows) are peculiar in that they have no reflection. The Count *knew* that he didn't look his best.

"As soon as we arrive back in civilisation," he announced out loud and to nobody in particular, "the item at the top of my shopping-list will be an electric iron."

With which remark, and with Skopka padding along at his side and Peppina dozing contentedly on his shoulder, Count Alucard set off across the warm, fine sand which was loose under his feet. The Count walked purposefully. He was in good spirits. He was proud of himself for the way in which he had coped with the previous night's happenings. First getting the better of a host of zoo-keepers and guards, then guiding the boat through a fearsome storm and finally escaping unscathed from a horrendous shipwreck. He had triumphed where many a braver man might have failed.

"I may have been at the back of the queue when courage was being doled out," he told himself. "But I think I can safely say that I accredited myself well last night – and that gives me great pleasure.

Arriving at the foot of the wooded slope, Count Alucard drew back his slim shoulders, lengthened his stride and raised his eyes towards the sumit. "When we arrive at the top," he said, glancing down at the young wolf by his side, "it will be downhill going from then on – to warm beds, good food and friendly ears eager to hear our tales of the heroic deeds and the brave adventures we have encountered."

"Alas, my friends, I sadly fear that there is no hope for us whatsoever!" wailed Count Alucard, as he sat down heavily on a clump of grass at the top of the hill – so heavily, in fact, that he jolted Peppina out of her doze, causing the parrot to flutter into the air, screeching raucous complaints. The courage that the Count had seemed to acquire at the foot of the hill had evaporated as quickly as it had come when the three companions reached the summit.

Count Alucard's sudden change of mood, from buoyant optimism to the very depths of despair, was not at all unusual. By nature, the Count was the sort of man who was either happy, or he was sad. There was seldom any "in-between". Nor did it take very much to get him from one of those conditions to the other.

These instant mood-swings are a characteristic, the Count will tell you, that he has inherited from his great-great-grandfather. For a while Count Alucard's father, and his father's father, were both down-to-earth Transylvanian noblemen, his father's father's father had been an entirely different sort of vampire. Count Alucard's great-great-grandfather (who had been known to the Tolokovinites as Alucard the Unexpected), had been a Transylvanian nobleman who might be dancing a jig on the roof of Castle Alucard at one moment then, half a minute later, be sitting sobbing his heart out in the deepest castle dungeon. Happily, the present Count was not as extreme in his switches of mood as his famous ancestor, but there can be no doubt as to which one of the previous Alucards he took after. And while the present Count might wish that he had not inherited his great-great-grandfather's failing, he gave thanks that he did not take after that particular forebear in another way – for Count Alucard the Unexpected had been a genuine, cold-hearted, out-and-out blood-drinking vampire.

"I suppose things *could* be worse than they are at present," Count Alucard sighed as he sat on his tuffet of grass and spoke to Skopka who was squatting on the ground in front of him. The reason for the Count's recent change of mood, from joy to gloom, was plain to see. "We're castaways, Peppina," he continued to the parrot as it fluttered back on to his shoulder. "We're shipwrecked on a desert island."

There was no denying the truth of this last statement. Looking down from the top of the hill, the view was more or less the same in every direction: wooded slopes, broken up with rocky outcrops, leading gently down to thicker woods below, with the occasional small valley, then the golden beach beyond, with here and there a tranquil bay – and then the shimmering, blue sea surrounding the island, stretching away, as far as the eye could see, to the empty encompassing horizon.

The vegetarian vampire sighed and his eyes widened as he considered what life would be like for himself and his companions as castaways on the island? What could they eat? Where would they sleep? Where should they shelter if another storm were to chance along? Another panicky thought came into Count Alucard's head: What about drinking water?

"Hopefully, we won't be here fore very long," the Count attempted to assure himself. "There's bound to be a ship passing this way in an hour or two – or an aircraft flying overhead. We will simply need to find a way of signalling to either one of those to come to our immediate rescue."

Although he had been talking to himself, Count Alucard had said the words aloud. Skopka, his head on one side, ears pricked, had given the Count his full attention. Despite the fact that he had not understood what the Count had said, the young wolf thumped his tail as if giving his approval. Peppina, on the other hand, had wandered up and down Count Alucard's shoulder, twitching her head and ruffling her neck feathers, and paying not the slightest heed to what he had to say.

"On the other hand, there is no knowing how far we sailed last night – or how much further the boat was carried in the teeth of that storm?" the Count continued in some concern. "We may have travelled well beyond the shipping lanes. It's possible that it could be days before a vessel comes this way? Perhaps a week? . . . Surely not a month? . . . Or even longer?"

And then a far more worrying thought entered Count Alucard's head. Supposing an aircraft did appear directly overhead, or a ship were to sail within hailing distance? How could he be sure that either the aircraft, or the boat, might not belong to the enemies they had escaped from the night before? In which case, Count Alucard argued to himself, wouldn't it be wiser for himself and his companions to hide, rather than draw attention to themselves?

"Something tells me," Count Alucard spoke aloud again as he scrambled to his feet, "that we are going to spend a longer time here than we might possibly care to?"

"*Olé!*" Peppina squawked then, spreading wide her wings, she launched herself from off Count Alucard's shoulder, soaring first out over the hill which fell away beneath her, then gliding downwards as she headed towards a grove of palm trees. As the parrot approached this chosen landing-spot, a number of small, yellow-chested finches flew up out of the palm trees' branches, chirruping, as if to greet her. A great deal had happened to Peppina since her escape from the zoo on the previous night, and at such a hectic pace that she had not had time to consider her freedom. This then, was the first real chance that the parrot had had to discover what life was like outside the wire-mesh strictures of a cage – she was enjoying it immensely.

"Peppina, at least, has no complaints with regard to her present whereabouts," Count Alucard observed, as he watched the parrot settle down amongst the flock of new-found friends. "Come along, Skopka," he continued, giving the young wolf a friendly pat. "Time to explore the island."

"On the whole, and taking one thing with another," Count Alucard announced later, on the afternoon of that same day and after the three shipwrecked companions had inspected their island, "we are not half so badly off as I had first feared."

Moving at a leisurely pace and stopping to linger over anything and everything that drew their interest or attention, the trek around the island had taken the three castaways about three hours in all. Count Alucard guessed, afterwards, that the desert island was about a mile and a half in length, and some three quarters of a mile across. For the most part, the Count was delighted at what they had discovered.

So far as shelter was concerned, the Count had stumbled upon a small cave, situated in a rock-face conveniently close to the foot of the hill and on that side of the island opposite the bay where the castaways had been washed ashore. It was not so much a cave, but more of a fissure in the rocks and not as deep as the Count would have liked. What's more, the floor was uncomfortably uneven – but it would provide *some* shelter in a storm, and once the floor had been covered with soft bracken, pliant twigs and fresh leaves, it would be soft enough to give Skopka a bed which he might sleep on, while there were plenty of nooks and crannies in the wall to make perching places for Peppina.

As for Count Alucard, without the cosy comfort of four coffin walls around him and lacking a coffin-lid to pull down over himself and shut out the cares of the world, sleep would not come to him easily – but he would look to his own needs later on that account.

On the food front, there was good news – at least for two of the castaways. Best of all, and much to Count Alucard's relief, drinking-water was not going to provide them with a problem. It was Skopka who had come across a fresh-water spring, while loping in the woods not far from the cave. Then, while the young wolf and the vegetarian vampire had been sampling the cool, clear water, Peppina's urgent squawking had drawn them to a nearby glade, bordered by hazel-nut trees and where wild strawberries carpeted the ground.

"*Bueno! Bueno!*" the parrot had screeched, as the Count and Skopka arrived on the scene.

"Excellent, well done, Peppina," Count Alucard had said. "This will more than suit us for the moment – and I have no doubt that we will find more varieties of fruit and berries in other parts of the island."

Although, while the Count and Peppina were well satisfied by this vegetarian diet, the meat-eating Skopka was not nearly so enthusiastic. The three of them were relaxing, on the grassy clearing outside the cave on that same afternoon. Peppina was feasting on a pile of nuts which the Count had shelled on her behalf, while he himself was dining on sweet, succulent strawberries, watched by a doleful wolf.

"Try some, Skopka," the vegetarian vampire urged, holding out a handful of strawberries to the wolf.

Skopka held back, his tail between his legs. "They might not be the kind of food that you are used to," the Count admitted, "but until we come across something more suited to your tastebuds, at least they'll provide you with sustenance. Come *on*, Skopka. The very least that you can do, is *try* them."

Skopka edged forward, one paw first and then another, until his nose was hovering over the fruit on offer in Count Alucard's open hand. The young wolf allowed his nostrils to sniff around and over the fruit. He opened his mouth, stuck out his tongue and hesitantly sucked in a couple of strawberries.

"That's the spirit!" Count Alucard exclaimed, as Skopka forced himself to gulp down the fruit. But the young wolf took two steps backwards hungry though he was, when the Count proffered him a second helping, shaking his head and whimpering his refusal.

The Count said nothing and ate the second handful of strawberries himself, but in his heart he knew that he would need to find something more suited to Skopka's palate. Although he was a vegetarian himself, he recognised that Skopka's needs were different from his own, and that they would have to be satisfied soon or else the wolf would start to suffer.

"Caramba!" squawked Peppina, who had been far too busy feeding on the hazel-nuts to notice what had been going on between Count Alucard and Skopka. *"Caramba!"* she squawked again, indicating that she had finished her first helping and was eager for a second.

Because of the hunger in his stomach, Skopka slept fitfully, twitching on the bed of twigs and leaves and bracken which Count Alucard had carefully prepared for him inside the cave. Peppina, having dined well on hazel-nuts and also slurped on a strawberry, slept soundly, perched on an overhanging rock shelf high up on the cave wall, her head sunk on her chest, her beak tucked away inside her breast feathers. The South American parrot was snoring softly.

Unable to sleep, partly because of his lack of a coffin and partly because he was concerned on Skopka's behalf, the Count was sitting in the mouth of the cave staring out at the moonlit night. He knew that the

same moon shone down on the Forest of Tolokovin, and he wished that he was home in the Castle Alucard, wrapped in his shroud and fast asleep in his favourite coffin. But there was no time now for thoughts of home, Count Alucard told himself as he clambered to his feet. An idea had occurred to the vegetarian vampire and he was going to put it into practice. After a backward glance inside the cave at where his two companions were sleeping, the vegetarian vampire strode out towards the centre of the grassy clearing.

Once there, Count Alucard put his black-shod feet together, heels touching, toe-caps slightly apart and took hold of the hem of his cloak in both hands, then raised his arms on either side of his body. The vegetarian vampire stood perfectly still, in that position, for several seconds, then closed his eyes, lifted his face towards the stars, took a deep breath and held it as the transformation began to happen. The Count's body seemed to tremble, then to shrivel, as his feet left the ground and, as he had done before on countless occasions, he made the change from human form to creature of the night.

Seconds later, the Count had flitted off into the dark. For ten minutes and more the vegetarian vampire soared high and low around the island, sometimes zig-zagging between the branches on the wooded slopes, sometimes darting upwards and skimming over the tallest tree-tops. For no matter how dejected or downcast Count Alucard might feel when he was in his human shape, his spirits always lifted when he changed into his other self. Whatever problems the world had to offer him when his feet were planted on the ground, seemed to melt away like snow in warm sunlight whenever he spread his browny-black membraneous wings and took off in flight.

But the Count had not come out that night purely for pleasure. He had left his two companions slumbering in the cave in order to carry out a task which he had set himself. Having enjoyed his solo flight enormously, he turned his snub bat's nose towards the sea and set out across the bay, skimming low, a bat's claw's width above the smooth, waters of the bay in which was mirrored the star-spangled sky.

9

"Things may not be half as bad as you imagine, Skopka," said Count Alucard, pausing as he rummaged around in the rocks by the shore on the morning after his moonlight flight, in an attempt to cheer up the young wolf.

Skopka, gnawing on a clump of grass at the edge of the beach, did not bother to so much as whimper in reply. By his calculations, he had not eaten proper food since the day before the day before the night that had just gone. Skopka was ravenously hungry. While the grass did not stave off the hunger pangs, his animal instinct told the wolf that the grass's juices would serve to keep his stomach in working order until real food came his way.

"*Bonito Peppina!*" squawked the parrot, strutting back and forth by the side of a rock-pool and pausing occasionally to admire her own reflection. Peppina had breakfasted well on nuts and berries and was not concerned about Skopka's hunger. "*Bonito Peppina!*" she repeated.

"It's 'pretty' Peppina, not 'bonito'," said the Count, translating the parrot's Spanish into English. If, as Count Alucard feared, their stay on the desert island might possibly stretch into weeks – or even months – the time would pass more pleasantly if Peppina and himself shared a common language.

"*Bonito Peppina!*" the parrot repeated, nodding her beak at her rock-pool image and ignoring what the vegetarian vampire had said.

"Ah-*WHER-wher-wherrrr*" whined Skopka, giving tongue to his self-pity.

Count Alucard sighed, then his spirits rose as he spotted what he had been looking for, wedged between a cleft in the rocks.

"Here we are!" the Count exclaimed, tugging first one, and then the second of the life-jackets free and waving them, one in either hand above his head. He had hidden the life-jackets in the rocks for safe-keeping the day before and, in his usual muddle-headed fashion, had promptly forgotten where he had put them. "How easy it is to fasten a life-jacket when you're standing with both feet on firm sand and not being bucketed about the deck of a boat in a raging gale," he told himself as he tied the life-jacket's strings neatly and in a bow this time around his middle. Then, turning to Skopka, he held out the second one, saying: "Here, boy! You're next."

Skopka backed away uneasily from the proffered life-jacket, his tail between his legs. The life-jacket only served to remind the wolf of the dark night, the pitching sea and the howling storm which he had suffered. Keeping his belly close to the sand, the young wolf edged backwards and away from the Count, whining softly.

"Suit yourself, Skopka, but I'm swimming out across the bay this morning, partly on your behalf, and I hoped that you'd accompany me." Count Alucard said crossly, then continued: "I made a preliminary inspection of the wreck, while you were asleep last night, and there are several things on board that boat – not least some tinned meats that would suit your stomach – which we could try and salvage before more rough seas come along and break up the craft entirely." He paused before adding: "What about you, Peppina? Do you feel like flying out there with me?"

Peppina, who was busy fluttering her wing-feathers in the rock-pool did not even bother to reply.

Count Alucard shook his head, then turned his back on his companions and strode out into the sea, which was calm, crystal-clear and warmly welcoming. After he had waded sufficiently far out to feel the water rising up around his armpits, he became aware of something splashing out in his direction. Glancing over his shoulder, Count Alucard was surprised at seeing Skopka heading out from shore, without a life-jacket but dog-paddling contentedly towards him. For while the Count's nervous disposition prevented him from entering any stretch of water (public bathing-pools included) without some sort of swimming-aid around his middle, the young wolf was a natural swimmer in calm water and fell in comfortably at the vegetarian vampire's side.

"Good wolf, Skopka!" Count Alucard said, as he moved out of his depth and began to execute a clumsy breaststroke. A moment later, the Count was even more delighted to discover that Peppina, too, had decided to accompany him and was hovering above the water not far from his head. "We shall survive this desert island castaway adventure," Count Alucard quietly assured himself as he struck out awkwardly

126

towards the wreck, "so long as we three remain good friends and tackle every obstacle together."

Two hours later, or thereabouts, Count Alucard was back on the beach, tired out from his exertions, but delighted at what he and his companions had managed to accomplish.

In his bat-self form, during the previous night's flight, the vegetarian vampire had discovered that, when the boat had been driven on to the rocks and shattered in two parts, one half of the craft had washed away.

The front part of the boat however, including most of the cabin, was still intact, part-sunk and rest-ing on a hidden shelf of rock. By attaching a length of ship's rope to a table-top which had come adrift and was floating inside the cabin, Count Alucard had managed to fashion a sort of simple raft which, with Skopka's assistance, they had been able to tow ashore, loaded with anything and everything that the Count considered might prove useful.

Count Alucard lowered himself on to the firm sand by the water's edge, and allowed his eyes to wander over the goods that had been salvaged from the wreck. Firstly, and most importantly, an abundance of tinned foodstuffs, much of which would go towards satisfying Skopka's needs, at least for the immediate future: tins of corned beef; tinned steak-and-kidney pies; tinned meat puddings; tinned meat-and-vegetable stew: tinned luncheon meat: several tins of frankfurters, and other meaty things besides.

The Count had also had the common sense to add a tin-opener to the list of things that he had sought during his trip to the shipwrecked boat out in the bay. Immediately, on the castaway's return to shore, Count Alucard had put the tin-opener to good use on one of the tinned steak-and-kidney pies over which Skopka was licking his chops and slobbering at that very moment.

There were other things, as well as foodstuffs, that the vegetarian vampire and his companions had brought back that morning: a length of stout sailcloth which, the Count reckoned, would come in handy as the roof of a shelter; a sewing kit; a coil of strong ship's rope; a magnifying-glass, which the Count had come across in a drawer containing charts and maps, and by which means and with the aid of the sun, he hoped to light a fire; a knife and fork; a red and white checked tablecloth and some paper napkins (for Count Alucard was a fastidious diner). Best of all was a large wooden box, which he had come across beneath a bunk, containing a set of joiner's tools: a saw; a hammer; a hatchet; a screwdriver, and several boxes of nails and screws.

In addition to all of the above, there had been one last thing that the Count had remembered spotting in the chart-drawer, and which he had collected before setting out back towards the shore: a brand-new hard-backed ship's log-book, together with some ballpoint pens.

"This empty book will come in very useful," Count Alucard murmured to himself as he flicked through the pages. He paused, then added: *"Very* useful indeed."

"A DESERT ISLAND DIARY" Count Alucard wrote the words carefully and importantly, in big capital letters, across the top of the first page of the log-book then sat back, stared out into the distance, sucked at the end of his ballpoint pen, and wondered what to put next?

It was the morning of the day after the day on which the three castaways had swum out to the shipwreck. They had just finished breakfast. The Count and Peppina had had fruit and nuts while Skopka had wolfed down half a tin of frankfurter sausages. Afterwards, the wolf had stared at the vegetarian vampire and tentatively wagged his tail, indicating that he could have easily swallowed the tin's entire contents, but Count Alucard had shaken his head. The Count had no idea how long they would be staying on the island, and while there was plenty for Peppina and himself, the tinned foods they had rescued from the shipwrecked boat would dwindle day by day.

Possibly, the Count told himself, there could be some sort of wildlife on the island which the young wolf might hunt down and certainly, there were all kinds of fish in the sea, but fishing was a skill that Skopka had yet to learn. Count Alucard, who was sit-

129

ting in the shade of some trees beyond the clearing, glanced across at where Skopka was hurtling round and round at high speed in a tight circle, in pursuit of his own tail. There was still some cub's playfulness in Skopka, but he would need to save all his energy for hunting, if he were going to survive.

"Buenos dias!" squawked Peppina, from off in the distance. Count Alucard shaded his eyes and peered across at where the South American parrot was headed back towards the grove of palm trees where the yellow-breasted finches nested. As before, the flock of birds rose up out of the branches at Peppina's approach.

"At least Peppina has managed to make some friends," Count Alucard told himself, and he turned his attention back to the log-book which was balanced in his lap. Again the vegetarian vampire sucked on the end of his pen and his brow wrinkled as he tried to collect his thoughts. At last, he began to write . . .

Three days have now passed since myself and my companions were cast up on this desert island and, in the unhappy event that rescue comes there none, I am resolved to keep this diary which shall serve to tell our story should some passing seafarer chance upon it in the years to come. Having examined the island thoroughly, I am convinced that there are no human folk inside its boundaries. There are, however, several species of bird-life and, hopefully, there may also be some sort of animal species (which has thus far chosen to remain hidden from our view) and which will serve to sustain poor Skopka (my young wolf companion) when his present food stocks are all gone. On which account, and without Skopka's knowing, I have decided to secretly mix in some vegetable matter with his meaty stuffs with the intention of making his tinned provisions last that much longer. As for myself and Peppina (the South American parrot who makes up our party) we shall do well enough for food as there are fruit, nuts and fresh water in plentiful supply. Though how we shall survive when winter comes, I scarcely dare to think. We are presently camped in a small cave on the South side of the island, but as these present quarters are open to both wind and weather, and having salvaged a box of tools from the shipwreck, I shall attempt my carpentering skills on building us a proper shelter with four walls and a roof. I am further resolved to put this last task at the very top of my list of priorities.

Signed
Count Alucard
(of Tolokovin, Transylvania)

"Clunk!" . . . "Clunk!" . . . "Clunk!" The sound of the hammer on nails echoed all across the island. It was late afternoon on the following day and Count Alucard had worked unceasingly, since first light that morning, at his self-appointed task.

"There! That should suffice," the vegetarian vampire told himself as he finished hammering. "And that is what I call a good job excellently executed," he added as he stepped back a pace and admired his ramshackle handiwork.

The Count had not, as yet, begun to build the shelter which he had himself put at the top of his "priorities" on the previous afternoon. He had spent the whole day, starting immediately after breakfast, constructing something which he had decided was even more important than a shelter. Count Alucard had just hammered home the very last nail into the coffin he had made for himself.

"After all," he said to Skopka and Peppina who had watched curiously as the Count had commenced his task, "if I haven't got a coffin, I simply cannot sleep a wink. And without a good night's sleep, my dears, I am absolutely hopeless in the mornings. I tell you, I am simply not fit to be spoken to – and certainly not in any sort of condition to even contemplate building us a shelter."

And so the coffin had replaced the shelter at the top of the "priorities" list. Skopka and Peppina had retired to a safe distance as Count Alucard had attacked a small tree with his hatchet and wood-chippings had begun to fly in all directions.

And now the coffin was built and ready for occupation. To be truthful, it did not look much like a coffin. To be absolutely honest, it did not really look like anything at all. The tree-bark was there to be seen on the rough-hewn planks which had been put together in higgledy-piggledy fashion. There were nails galore which had been knocked in wrongly, sticking out in all directions – the Transylvanian nobleman was no dabhand when it came to carpentry. His latest handiwork had four walls, a bottom, and lid which opened and closed – after a fashion on sailcloth hinges. And, because it was the most difficult thing he had attempted in the whole of his life, Count Alucard was proud of himself.

"I'll admit that it might not *look* comfortable," the Count said to Skopka, as the young wolf padded forward and sniffed inquisitively at the fresh wood smell of the coffin. "But once the floor's been covered with

132

leaves and grass," the Count continued to Peppina, who had fluttered across and was parading along the rim of the coffin's lid, "I shall be as comfortable as a wood-louse in a rotting oak-apple."

"*Olé!*" squawked the parrot, stretching her wings.

Meanwhile, Skopka had lifted his head, craned his neck, opened wide his mouth, and had begun to howl loud and long at the moon which was edging up, over the horizon, into the darkening sky. Having lost all interest in Count Alucard's rustic-work coffin, the young wolf was already wondering about what he would be getting for supper.

Count Alucard sighed contentedly, eased his body on to the soft bed of greenery which covered the bottom of the coffin, and flicked through the pages of *The Coffin-Maker's Journal*. It was a warm, clear night. So warm, in fact, that the Count had decided to leave his coffin out on the clearing – and so clear that he was able to read his favourite magazine by the moon's bright light.

Skopka and Peppina had also opted to sleep out in the open. The young wolf was curled up comfortably, his nose tucked close to his stomach, in a little hollow in the ground by the foot of the coffin, while the South American parrot had chosen a perch on the lowest branch of a nearby tree. Skopka, having had a hard day of it, mostly going round and round in pursuit of his own tail and without success, was fast asleep already. Peppina, on the other hand, had done little or nothing of any exertion, apart from paying her courtesy visit to her new-found friends, the flock of finches, and was still awake, her beak sunk into her breast-feathers, gazing at the Count, unblinking.

Count Alucard turned another page. He had read the much-thumbed copy of that month's issue of *The Coffin-Maker's Journal* so many times, he now knew every word of it by heart while every illustration was committed to his memory. The pages which he turned to now were the last ones in the journal, and both of them were given over to advertisements. All of these ads were to do with coffins and most of them were accompanied by pictures. There were pictures of coffins made from all sorts of wood, and with different kinds of handles – from the cheapest pinewood coffin with plain brass handles, and insides lined with padded cotton, to the most expensive types of caskets, fashioned from African teak or Canadian maple, with filigreed silver handles and interiors covered with the finest silk and padded with the softest swansdown.

The Count's black, beady eyes wandered, for the umpteenth time over both of these pages, taking in the vast selection of undertakers' furnishings and funereal items. Although, in spite of the amazing range of coffins that the magazine had on offer, the vegetarian vampire could honestly state that, on that particular warm island evening, lying under the canopy of stars and with the full moon's kindly face beaming down on him from a black velvet sky, he would not have swapped the comfort of the simple coffin he had made himself for any one of the models advertised in *The Coffin-Maker's Journal.*

Hip-hip-hurrah! began the entry set down in Count Alucard's spidery handwriting in his log-book diary. *We have been shipwrecked for two weeks exactly and this morning Skopka succeeded in catching his very first fish! I had been strolling along the beach, with Peppina for company on my shoulder, looking for driftwood (which I have discovered, when dried in the sun and chopped into small pieces, provides excellent kindling for a fire) when all at once I heard a splashing and a commotion coming from the sea's direction. Lo and behold, turning my eyes to look, I spotted Skopka standing up to his belly in the water, thrashing his tail to-and-fro in pleasure and pride – and with his first fish dinner clamped firmly between his teeth. Upon sight of which, I fell down on my knees on the sand and gave thanks to St Unfortunato for the tins of meaty stuffs are nearly at an end. Howsoever, if Skopka can continue to improve his fishing prowess, then we have nothing to fear (at least so long as this late summer continues) for as far as Peppina and myself are concerned, this little island is a veritable treasure-trove of delicious things to eat . . . Alas though, while our time spent on the island leaves little to be desired, we cannot stay here indefinitely – but so far as our being rescued goes there is no good news in that particular direction. In all the time that we have been here thus far, there has been neither sight nor sound of any aircraft, and although I did on one occasion catch sight of a ship, the vessel was so far off in the distance that I cannot be absolutely sure that it was not my own eyesight playing tricks on me. As the days and weeks go by, it is becoming all too clear that, if we are to survive the winter, then I must begin work on a proper shelter before the bad weather comes along.*

Having worked unceasingly all day, Count Alucard paused to take stock of all that he had done. He had not, as yet, begun work on the hut that he planned to build and which would serve to protect himself and his companions through the harsh winter weather. He had been far too busily engaged on another task which he had decided was of equal, if not greater, importance.

Since first light that morning, the vegetarian vampire had sat, cross-legged, on the grass outside the cave, snipping away with the scissors he had come across in the sewing-kit. After which, he had stitched and sewed, tacked and trimmed and, at last, his endeavours were complete. Count Alucard had made himself a new jacket, a new pair of trousers, and a new cloak – all out of sailcloth.

Originally, when he had salvaged the sailcloth from the wreck out in the bay, and brought it safely back to shore, the Count had intended that he would use the material to make a roof for the shelter. But he had put that idea to the back of his mind when it had occurred to him that it could be put to a far better purpose by being turned into a new suit of clothes.

If Count Alucard had listened to the small, urgent voice of reason inside his head, he would have heard it tell him that building a shelter against the coming winter was far, far more important than his having a choice of things to wear. By nature, the vegetarian vampire was a bit of a dandy and (like most dandies) he seldom listened to reason when he was shopping for new clothes. It should be said, on his behalf, that the suit he was presently wearing *was* showing grave signs of wear and tear after the length of time spent on the island, to say nothing of the wrinkles and the shrinkage it had suffered from the time spent, after the shipwreck, in the sea.

Back home in Castle Alucard, on Tolokovin Mountain, in Transylvania, Count Alucard had a whole row of suits hanging side-by-side in a big oak walk-in wardrobe in his bedroom. The suits were all identical in style and cut and size and black in colour. Also, he had a massive chest-of-drawers, standing next to the wardrobe, which was full to bursting with starched white shirts, white silk underpants and vests, and black silk socks neatly tucked in pairs. There was an entire row of shiny black pairs of shoes on the wardrobe floor and any number of white bow ties hanging on a silken cord behind the wardrobe door. When he was resident in his castle, there was nothing that the Count enjoyed quite so much as dressing every morning in neatly ironed and smartly pressed fresh clothing (despite the fact that this new attire was exactly the same, in every single detail, as the clothing he had worn the day before). Best of all, when he was fully dressed, Count Alucard took much delight in primping, preening and admiring himself in the wardrobe's full-length mirror.

Here on the island, all the clothing that the Count possessed were the items he had been wearing when he was shipwrecked.

"Getting up in the morning, on this desert island, would be *so* much easier, if only I had some other clothes to choose from," Count Alucard had told himself as he had lain in the comfort of his rough-hewn coffin early that morning, trying to raise the energy to face the day ahead. Then, after letting out a long, sad sigh, he had shrugged his slim shoulders, fluttered his long fingers in front of his face, and continued: "As things stand at this particular moment, there is no pleasure whatsoever in dragging oneself to one's feet and having to put on the same *boring* garments, day after day.

And so, instead of starting work on the much-needed shelter, the vegetarian vampire had laboured away from dawn till dusk, at making himself a brand new suit of clothes. Now that he had completed his task, and both the jacket and the trousers were laid out neatly on the ground, Count Alucard stood for several minutes, tapping a forefinger on his chin and gazing down, proudly, at what he had accomplished. At last, the Count stopped, picked up both garments, and strolled into the cave.

Skopka and Peppina both soon returned after Count Alucard had gone into the cave. They had quickly tired, shortly after breakfast, of watching the Count's fingers busy with the scissors, needle and thread, and had gone off, in different directions and on separate business. Peppina to pass the time of day with the flock of finches; Skopka to see if he could repeat his previous day's success at fishing (sadly, he had been unlucky). They had returned, coincidentally, at one and the same time, when their stomachs had reminded them that supper-time was not too far away.

When Count Alucard stepped out of the cave wearing his new suit of clothes, Skopka was squatting on his haunches on the grass in front of the cave, while Peppina had found a convenient perch on an overhanging rock.

"Well?" said the vegetarian vampire, giving a little twirl and then posturing in front of his companions. "What do you think?"

It was an awkward question.

Neither the jacket nor the trousers looked quite right. In the first place, the sailcloth was too stiff and coarse to be turned into clothing, in the second place, the Count had not done a good job at fashioning the rough material into a suit. Neither of the garments fitted him: the jacket was too long and baggy; the trousers were too short and far too tight. The Count was not to blame. He had never before tried his hand at tailoring. Separately, the garments looked a mess. Together, on the Count, they looked even worse. But because he had carefully cut them out and diligently stitched them together by himself, and in exactly the same way that he was proud of the coffin he had put together, Count Alucard was equally delighted with his homemade sailcloth jacket and trousers. He was similarly proud of his sailcloth cloak.

Skopka and Peppina, on the other hand, were not at all impressed.

"Dios mio!" squawked the South American parrot – which, in English, means "Goodness gracious!"

"Ah-WHOOO-ooo-oooooh!" went the Transylvanian wolf, letting out a disdainful wail.

"Please yourselves!" snapped the vegetarian vampire, giving a little sniff. "I happen to think myself that I cut quite a dash."

"Olé!" screeched Peppina, stretching her wings and with a twinkle in her eye.

"Ah-WHUFF!" went Skopka, pretending to sneeze as he tried, without succeeding, to hide his amusement at the Count's odd appearance.

Aware that both of his companions regarded him as a figure of fun, the Count turned his back on them and stomped off, sulkily, into the cave. Only a few minutes passed however, before Count Alucard reappeared, humming the tune of a lively Transylvanian folk-song, and began to prepare the evening meal as if nothing at all had happened. It might not have taken much to make the vegetarian vampire throw a sulk – but at least his sulks were never long-lasting.

As things turned out, the matter of the Count's attempts at tailoring and his companions' attitudes towards it, would prove of small importance compared to the astonishing discovery which they were to make in only a few days time.

10

It was Skopka who first discovered the footprint on the beach.

The young wolf was scampering along, early one morning and in zig-zag fashion, pausing briefly to sniff at the occasional crab or landbound starfish, when he suddenly stopped short. There, in the sand, some several metres in front of him, was the clear impression of a man's large footprint.

"What is it, Skopka?" Count Alucard called. The vegetarian vampire had been ambling along the beach some distance behind when he caught sight of the young wolf, half-crouched, ears pricked and with his nose twitching as it pointed along the beach. "Stay there! Stay still! Wait for me!" the Count instructed as he hastened to discover what it was that had excited Skopka's attention.

When the Count caught up with the young wolf, he too stood stock still for several seconds. Then, after taking in the footprint ahead, he gazed around, in every direction, in case the man who had made the impression in the sand might still be in the vicinity! But the beach and wooded slopes beyond seemed as devoid of human life as they had ever done and the Count decided that the coast was clear enough for him to give the footprint his full and close attention.

As Count Alucard took the few short necessary paces forward to bring him to the footprint, Skopka edged forward also, paw by paw and with his belly close to the ground. Then, as the vegetarian vampire dropped down on one knee in order to examine the strange discovery, the young wolf circled the imprint twice before sniffing, hesitantly, all around its edges.

It was not so much a footprint, the Count had realised, but more in the nature of a boot-print – and, without any doubt at all, made by a bigger boot than any item of footwear that Count Alucard had ever laid eyes on. The imprint was some thirty centimetres from heel to toe and, at its broadest point, almost half that length across. Whatever person fitted the boot must have been almost giant-sized.

"And of a weight to match, Skopka," the Count murmured nervously to his four-legged companion. "For look how deep the print goes into the sand. Why, you can even see the marks made by the boot-nails all around the sole!" As he spoke, the Count clambered back on to his feet and, once again, allowed his eyes to peer across at the nearby rocks and, also, into the fringe of trees. But there was neither sight nor sound of any other living creature.

"H-h-h-hello?" The Count called out nervously into the trees. Then, on receiving no reply, he turned towards the rocks and called out for a second time. "*Hello?* Is anyone there?" Again there was no answer.

The vegetarian vampire shivered – despite the fact that it wasn't cold. If the person who had made the boot-print *was* watching him, either through the trees or from behind a boulder, why didn't he reply? Perhaps because he was no longer there? In which case, where had he got to? And, equally important, where had he come *from*? And, most important of all, *why* had he come? Surely not in friendship, the Count told himself, or he would certainly have introduced himself by now.

"*Caramba!*"

Count Alucard jumped as Peppina, who had just arrived on the scene, skimmed past him, at knee height, and flew over the boot-print. Then, without pausing to give the print a full inspection, the parrot banked steeply, heading upwards from the beach and took up a perch on the topmost branch of the nearest tree.

"*Caramba!*" the parrot squawked again, with more assurance than before and sensing that she was safe from danger.

"*Ah-wher-wher-wher-wher!*" whimpered Skopka, wishing that he, too, was able to fly, or had learned to scramble, out of harm's way, up a tree.

"There, there, Skopka. Easy now," said the Count, trying hard not to let his voice give away the fact that he was just as frightened as his companion. "Whoever made that bootprint in the sand is not around here at the moment – and, when he does return, I don't intend to be around to greet him. Come along!"

With which, Count Alucard turned on his heel and set off, running awkwardly through the soft sand and up the beach, then through the undergrowth into the shelter of the trees and thence up the slope towards the safety of the cave which was on the other side of the hill. Skopka followed close on the vegetarian vampire's heels.

"*Olé!*" squawked Peppina from the safety of her

tree, as she watched her friends set off. After the Count and Skopka had gone, and she could no longer hear them crashing through the trees, Peppina took stock of her surroundings. She was, she knew, in no danger whatsoever on the tree-top and to prove to herself that she had no fears, Peppina shuffled up and down the branch, then spread her wings and preened the spot underneath her left wing where it was attached to her body.

"Buenos dias!" screeched the parrot, with a flutter. But there was nothing except silence on her every side – a strange and empty silence that made Peppina's feathers itch and caused her to wonder whether someone might be watching her. All at once, Peppina missed the company of her friends.

Thrusting her body upwards, Peppina launched herself into the air and, skimming over the tops of the trees, she flew, straight as an arrow, towards the cave.

When Count Alucard and Skopka arrived back at the cave, Skopka first and then the Count panting from his exertions, they found that Peppina had got there before them and was perched on a favourite ledge on the rock-face above the entrance.

"Hola!" screeched the parrot, bobbing her balding head in welcome to her companions.

But the Count was far too concerned at the discovery on the beach to respond to Peppina's greeting, and far too tired, having loped on his long legs all the way back to the cave, to do anything except flop down on the grass and gulp in deep breaths of air. Skopka, too, ignored the parrot's "Hello!". Instead, the young wolf padded into the cave, curled up on the bed of leaves, promptly fell asleep and dreamed of a world that was overrun with rabbits.

Two full weeks have now gone by since we sighted the foot-print in the sand, Count Alucard wrote, in his careful spidery handwriting, in his diary, *and although we have searched every square metre of this island, and every one of its nooks and crannies, we have failed to make contact with the big-booted being that left his mark on the beach – or, indeed, to find further evidence of his present presence on the island.*

Setting down both pen and diary on the grass beside him, the Count clambered to his feet, crossed to the fire, picked up a log and tossed it on to the glowing embers, causing a shower of crackling sparks to shoot up, in the wood-smoke, and head towards the dark night sky. The newly-added log took fire instantly and long tongues of red and orange flame lit up the castaways' camp-site outside the cave.

Only a week or so ago, the vegetarian vampire would have worried that such a blaze would give away his exact location to the mysterious, big-booted being, but the nights were growing chillier and the Count, who liked his creature comforts, had decided to throw caution to the winds. "In any case," he told himself, "if the intruder was intent on harming either myself or my companions, wouldn't he have snatched at an opportunity already, while we were busy at our day-to-day chores and off-guard?" Another thought which had recently occurred to the Count was that the person who had left the footprint might have also left the island? "Is it not possible, nay, more than likely," the Count argued to himself, "that the mysterious big-booted one came here by boat, possibly under the cover of darkness and, not finding what he was after, put out to sea again immediately?"

Settling himself down again in front of the blazing fire, Count Alucard picked up the ship's log and wrote his latest theory down. Then, having done so, he read over what he had just written. It was a possibility which pleased the vegetarian vampire. For if it was true, then he and his companions were not in any danger. And, because the idea appealed to him, the Count was inclined to believe it.

Later that same night though, while both his companions lay sound asleep, with Skopka's flanks rising and falling to the gentle rhythm of Peppina's soft snores, Count Alucard lay wide awake in his rough-hewn coffin and gazed up, unblinking, at the starry sky. A worrying thought had entered Count Alucard's head and he was finding sleep hard to come by. For if his latest theory *was* correct, and the large-booted being *had* come and gone by boat, then there was no reason why he could not come back again and, should he choose to do so, was it not also possible that he might not come alone? Try as he might, Count Alucard could not get the disturbing thought to go away.

"Don't move! Stand perfectly still – and don't look round!" the unexpected voice rang out at Count Alucard's back, as he stood high up on the rocky promontory, gazing out to sea.

The Count did as the voice had ordered. He did not move so much as a hair on his head. He kept himself as still as the statue of Saint Unfortunato, the patron saint of Tolokovin, which stood in that town's market square and which had not moved a millimetre in two hundred years and more. If the man who had barked out the order was the same man whose right foot fitted the giant-sized boot that had made the imprint in the sand, then the vegetarian vampire did not intend to quarrel with the fellow. Instead, he wondered if it might be possible to make friends?

"As a matter of fact, my dear good chap—" the Count began without daring to look round.

"And don't speak either!" the voice commanded. "You will do exactly as I say, for your own sake, and stand perfectly still and hold your silence!"

Count Alucard's slim shoulders drooped a little, but not sufficient, he made sure, for his assailant to notice. The vegetarian vampire sighed under his breath, and blamed himself for his predicament – if only he had taken more care when he had come through the trees.

Having lain awake most of the night, the Count had come down to the rocks at first light, leaving his companions sound asleep, in order to assure himself that his fears about a boat arriving had been unfounded.

Alas, it seemed now as if his worst nightmare had come true. A boat must have sailed in while he had been lying in his coffin, and anchored in another bay. Also, during the night, the crew had crept ashore and now one of them was standing just behind him – for Count Alucard was aware of the newcomer's approach and could feel the stranger's breath on the back of his neck.

Without daring to move his head, Count Alucard allowed his eyes to glance down, over the edge of the cliff at where the sea was washing on the sharp-edged rocks below. If the man who was standing just behind were to push him, hard, in the small of his back, the Count knew that he would tumble over the edge and . . . it was far too awful a thought for him to consider.

"You can turn round now," the voice told the Count.

Count Alucard turned – slowly, just to be on the safe side – and found himself looking into the eyes of a thin-faced man wearing a monocle and whose face was level with his own. "At least," the Count was able to reassure himself, "I am not looking *up* into the eyes of the large-size person who left the bootprint in the sand."

"See this!" said the stranger, breaking in on Count Alucard's thoughts and holding up, carefully, between finger and thumb, a wriggling hairy spider. "He was crawling across your shoulder. If you had moved your head or made a noise, this unattractive little fellow might very easily have scuttled down your neck."

"Was that why you called out to me?" asked the Count, as he gave a shudder at the very idea of having a hairy spider roaming around inside his clothing.

"Of course. Why else would I have called to you behind your back?"

"Then I'm extremely obliged to you," said the vegetarian vampire. "I simply cannot stand the sight of spiders. I've only so much as to glimpse one in the bath and it's enough to put me off my ablutions for the rest of the day."

"I'm not particularly fond of them myself," said the man then, after stooping down on one knee, he set the spider down, gently, on the ground. "But I am of the opinion that they have as much right to go about their business as any of God's other creatures."

"Oh, I do *so* agree", said the Count. Then, as the newcomer watched the spider zig-zag off across the rocks, the vegetarian vampire studied the man's clothing. "How odd!" he told himself. "He's dressed exactly as I would be dressed myself – were it not for the fact that my shipwreck circumstances have reduced me to wearing sailcloth suiting."

It was true. The man who had just rescued Count Alucard from the attentions of an inquisitive spider was wearing clothing strikingly similar to that which the Count chose to put on when he was home in his Transylvanian castle: black formal jacket and matching trousers: black shiny shoes; black silk socks; starched white frilly-fronted shirt; neatly tied white bow tie; and a long black cloak with a scarlet lining draped over his shoulders.

"Perhaps the time has come," began the newcomer, rising quickly to his feet as he realised that the Count was studying his appearance, "for us to introduce ourselves?"

"I was about to make that very suggestion myself,"

said the vegetarian vampire, adding: "You first?"

"No, after *you*," said the well-dressed stranger.

"My name is 'Alucard'," the vegetarian vampire said, proudly. Then, as he continued, he drew himself up to his full height. His ill-fitting sailcloth jacket hung all the more loosely on his slim body; his badly made sailcloth trousers looked that much shorter on his lanky legs. "I am *Count* Alucard, of Castle Alucard, which is situated on Tolokovin Mountain, in Transylvania."

"Delighted to make your acquaintance, Count," replied the newcomer. Then, giving the Count a brief nod of his head and, at the same time, clicking the heels of his well-polished shoes together, he added: "and my name is Frankenstein – Baron Frankenstein, from the country of Versaria."

"*Frankenstein!*" cried Count Alucard, taking a step backwards from the stranger. "Then you're the man that made the monster that goes round terrorising honest peasant folk!"

"Fiddlesticks – you've been listening to common gossip," snapped the well-dressed man, placing his monocle back in his eye and gazing through it, coldly, at the Count. "And you, sir – if you'll forgive me for saying so – are a fine one to talk, when it comes to terrorising simple peasants."

"I don't know what you mean," protested the Count, shuffling his feet uneasily.

"Oh yes you do!" scoffed Baron Frankenstein. "'Alucard'? Is that what you choose to call yourself?"

"It's my name," the Count said, crossly.

"No, it isn't. 'Alucard' is 'Dracula' spelled backwards. 'Alucard' indeed! Why, the very instant that you said the name out loud, I realised who you were. If I'd have had my wits about me, I'd have recognised you the moment I set eyes on you. Those pointy teeth, the red-rimmed eyes and that pale complexion are an instant giveaway. I have to admit that the sailcloth suit disguise did have me fooled for a little while. Well, at least I'm honest enough to tell you my real name. I don't go around pretending to be someone else. I may have been born a Frankenstein, but I'm certainly not ashamed of it. And, what's more, I don't go around in the dead of night, turned into a vampire bat and leaving teeth-marks in people's necks and draining all the blood from their bodies." Baron Frankenstein paused, pulled a face at the thought of quaffing human blood. "*Ugh!*" he went. "The very idea!" he added, with a shiver.

"For your information," the Count said, coldly. "I happen to be a total vegetarian."

"That's your story."

"It's *true*! But if it comes to talk of terrorising simple folk, according to the stories that I've heard, the peasants of Versania daren't allow *their* children out to play in daylight hours. They live their entire lives in constant dread of Frankenstein's monster."

"Which just goes to show that *some* fools will believe any old nonsense," replied the Baron, tartly. He paused, examined his fingernails, one by one, cleared his throat, twice, and then after raising his eyebrows enquiringly continued: "Er . . . by the way, speaking of monsters – you wouldn't have happened to have spotted one this morning, by any remote chance, wandering about the island?"

"*Aargh-eeh-OWWW!*"

The unearthly wail, unlike any sound that the Count had ever heard, came drifting down the side of the hill, through the trees on the morning air.

"My monster!" cried Baron Frankenstein, alarmed. "That's the cry he makes when he's in danger."

"*Ah-whoo-OOOOOOH!*" Skopka's howl of terror came immediately after and from the same direction.

"My wolf!" Count Alucard let out a horrified gasp, the added: "That's the way he howls when he's in serious trouble."

Pausing only long enough for each man to scowl in the other's direction, the two set off, as fast as their long legs would carry them, running hard in the direction from which the cries had come.

11

"Ah-whoo-OOOOOOH!"

"Aargh-eeh-OWWW!"

I'm warning you, Count Alucard," the Baron panted as the two men matched each other, stride for stride, first plunging through the undergrowth then racing through the trees in the direction from which the fearful howls and screams were coming. "If your wolf takes so much as a nip at my monster, you'll find yourself in very *very* hot water."

"And take heed yourself," the Count replied, struggling to catch his breath as he scowled across at Baron Frankenstein, "if your monster harms one hair on Skopka's body, you'll be the one that suffers for it."

"Aargh-eeh-OWWW!"

"Ah-whoo-OOOOOOH!"

Then, as they drew nearer to the clearing where the cave was situated, they were also able to hear the constant cries made by a third creature:

"Caramba! Caramba! Caramba! Caramba! Caramba!"

"Who's that screeching in Spanish?" gasped Baron Frankenstein.

"That's my parrot," Count Alucard panted fiercely. "And if a single one of that bird's feathers is damaged,

I shall see to it that you answer personally for your monster's misdeeds."

However, having raced the last few yards and arrived at the clearing together, both men realised that neither Skopka, Peppina, nor the monster had come to any harm – nor were they likely to, despite the combined racket they were making.

Frankenstein's monster, his back against the rockface, was waving his arms, wildly, and kicking out at nothing with his enormous booted feet, wailing and bellowing all the while in frustration at the young wolf and the parrot, both of whom, it should be said, were doing little more than tease him. Skopka was howling unceasingly in the monster's face but only from a very safe distance. Peppina, meanwhile, was hovering airborne and out of harm's way from the flailing arms, but keeping up a constant screeching which served to torment the monster all the more.

"*Aarg-eeh-OWWW!*" roared the outraged monster, his back against the rock.

"*Ah-whooo-OOOOOOH!*" howled Skopka, angered by the monster's cries but fearing to venture closer for fear of making contact with the monster's boots.

"*Caramba! Caramba! Caramba!*" taunted Peppina, fluttering above the monster's head, but always staying out of reach of his wildly swinging fists.

"Keep that monster quiet – and tell him to stand still!" Count Alucard called across at Baron Frankenstein, adding: "Can't you see that he's upsetting my companions?"

"Call off that stupid wolf and tell your silly parrot to behave herself!" snapped Baron Frankenstein in reply.

"Isn't it plainly obvious that they're tormenting my poor monster?"

In the heat and anger of the moment, each blamed the other for the unfortunate situation and, therefore, neither the Count nor the Baron felt it his duty to bring the rowdy altercation to an end. Finally, however, the deafening row got the better of both men and it was the vegetarian vampire that was the first to crack.

"For goodness sake, Skopka!" cried the Count, covering his ears with both his hands. "Do stop that infernal howling!"

"Stop bellowing, Monster!" shouted the Baron as he, too, attempted to blot out the din by covering up his ears.

"You too, Peppina!" the Count continued. "We'll have an end to that screeching, if you please."

"And put those fists down," Baron Frankenstein commanded the monster, adding: "And do stop kicking out – you'll end up hurting somebody, and then you *will* be sorry."

"That goes for all of you!" Count Alucard shouted, adding in his loudest voice: "Stand *STILL!*"

All three of the combatants got the message. Immediately, and blissfully, there was total silence or what would do for total silence after the bedlam that had gone before. Pepppina took herself off to the lowest branch of the nearest tree where, turning her back on everyone, she perched and preened her tail-feathers as if she had had nothing whatsoever to do with what had gone before. Skopka dropped his tail between his legs then, whimpering softly, turned round three times before settling himself on the grass outside the entrance to the cave. The monster mean-while, as though ashamed of his own part in the argument, allowed his arms to hang by his side, then hung his head and seemed to study his enormous boots.

In the calm that followed, the Count took the opportunity to study the monster for the first time. Secretly, the Count felt rather proud of both Skopka and Peppina for having dared to challenge the creature, for it really was a fearsome sight.

Standing well over two metres in height, it towered over Count Alucard who was himself taller than most men. The Count gasped as he considered the monster's size. The creature was of a build to match his height, with bulky shoulders and bulging muscles that tugged at the seams of the simply cut home-sewn jacket and trousers he was wearing. He had large, clumsy-looking hands and dark, gloomy, deepset eyes that peered out from underneath a bulging forehead which was part-covered by a thick fringe of black hair. There were two iron bolts, one on either side of the monster's neck and which were used as attachments when the monster was re-charged with electricity drawn, during violent thunderstorms, from lightning flashes. Count Alucard knew all about these things for he had read several scholarly, leather-bound books about the monster, which were kept on the library shelves at Alucard Castle. The Count allowed his eyes to wander all down the monster's massive frame and, finally, come to rest on the enormous hobnailed boots – there could be no doubt whatsoever in the vegetarian vampire's mind that it had been one of those large items of footwear that had left the imprint in the sand.

"His appearance quite belies his nature." The

159

Baron's voice broke in softly, on Count Alucard's thoughts. "He may *look* extremely dangerous," the Baron continued, "but underneath that fierce exterior, he is as gentle as any pussy-cat."

Count Alucard made no reply. He felt a sudden surge of pity for the sad-faced, awkward creature and was at a total loss for words. Baron Frankenstein misunderstood the vegetarian vampire's silence.

"I suppose, like all mankind, you don't believe what I have told you?" said Baron Frankenstein, with a long, sad sigh.

"Oh, but I do! I do! Indeed I do!" Count Alucard had suddenly found his tongue. "You may have my hand upon it, Baron, I believe every word that you have told me. Why, I myself suffer from the very same problem as your monster. I, too, am forced to endure the hatred of most of the human race – and, in my own case, all because of the misdeeds of my ancestors."

"Look here," said the Baron, pointing out towards the bay, "my boat is moored just off the coast. Why don't you come out, this evening, and join us for a spot of dinner?"

"I would really, *really* like to do that," Count Alucard replied, nodding eagerly.

"Then be there on the sand at sunset – I shall send across my manservant in the rowing-boat to collect you. His name is Igor."

"I don't suppose . . ." the Count began, his voice trailing off as he glanced down at the drowsing Skopka, and then across at Peppina who was still busy at her preening.

"What is it?"

"May I beg a favour?"

"Ask away?"

"I was wondering if you'd have any great objection to me bringing my companions with me?"

"My dear, dear fellow," Baron Frankenstein began, then taking his monocle out of his right eye he polished it briskly on his sleeve as he continued: "I wouldn't countenance your leaving them behind. "Why, not only do you have my permission to bring them, I *insist* that they come along."

"Wait!" cautioned the Count. "Before I accept your most generous offer, perhaps I should warn you that we are not the easiest guests to feed."

"And pray tell me, Count Alucard, why would that be?"

"I'm afraid we're rather fussy folk at table," the Count confessed with an apologetic little smile. "For while Peppina and myself are vegetarian by nature, Skopka is as carnivorous an animal as they come."

"Of course he is! 'course he is!" the Baron answered with a chuckle. "He's a wolf, is he not? What else would one expect of him?"

Skopka, while still stretched out on the ground, had had one eye open for some time and, as if understanding what had been said, thumped his tail down hard, three times.

"Believe me, Count Alucard," the Baron continued, "your eating habits are no different from our own, for while I myself am inclined to over indulge myself with cuts of meat, the monster here, like yourself, is strictly a fruit and vegetable chap."

The monster, as though embarrassed at having such a private matter as his eating habits discussed in public, hung his head and pretended to examine the toe-caps on his boots.

"Well I never!" said the Count.

"And so you see," the Baron added, "between the six of us, we shall make ideal dinner-table companions."

"Six?" said the Count, doing a hasty mental head-count and arriving at the figure five.

"I do beg your pardon, there is something that I quite forgot to mention," said the Baron. "My manservant, Igor, always joins the monster and myself at mealtimes – I take it that, despite your aristocratic upbringing, you would have no objection to that arrangement?"

"Good gracious, no!"

"Excellent!" cried Baron Frankenstein, clapping his hands together. "Then we shall be six at table and I have no doubt whatsoever that we shall enjoy our-selves enormously."

"I'm looking forward to the occasion," said the Count.

"Just one small thing," replied the Baron, "I'm afraid I have a head similar to a sieve – tell me again the names of your companions?"

"This young fellow's called 'Skopka'," said Count Alucard, indicating the wolf then, nodding across at the preening parrot, he added: "And that dear lady's name is 'Peppina'."

"Peppina!" screeched the parrot, fluttering her wings. "Peppina!" "Peppina!" "Peppina!"

"Pep – pina," it was the monster that repeated the name, slowly and carefully, splitting into two separate parts.

"He talks?" Count Alucard said, in some surprise,

for although the monster had watched attentively during all of the foregoing conversation, he had made no attempt to join in with it.

"Not very often, for he seldom has the opportunity to add to his vocabulary. I lack the time to talk him him on board the yacht, while Igor is not one for conversation. He does seem to have taken a liking to your parrot, though."

"Pep – pina," the monster said again, only louder this time and with more assurance.

"Peppina!" squawked the parrot in reply and, spreading her wings, she launched herself upwards, coming to rest a moment later on the monster's broad left shoulder. "*Caramba!*" she screeched on landing.

"Car – ram – ba!" echoed the monster, carefully and slowly.

"Do you wish to know what I think?" said the Count as he watched while Peppina high-strutted back and forth along her new-found perching-place. "Not only has your monster taken a liking to Peppina, but it's my opinion that Peppina's also taken quite a fancy to the monster. What's his name, by the way?"

"He is called 'Monster'," said the Baron with a shrug.

"Mon – ster," the creature repeated, hearing his name spoken aloud.

"It's the only name that he has ever cared to answer to," said the Baron. "He's had it since the first day he was put together."

The two men fell silent as they watched the monster raise his huge left hand and then poke his forefinger, ever so gently, close to Peppina's face. In return, the parrot nuzzled her beak against the monster's outstretched finger.

"Pep – pina," murmured the monster.

"*Olé!*" squawked Peppina.

"I believe that you're right, Count," said Baron Frankenstein. "They do appear to have taken a liking to each other."

Giving Count Alucard a friendly wave, Baron Frankenstein set off across the clearing with the monster at his side and with Peppina still perched, contentedly, on the monster's shoulder. It was not until the trio were halfway across the clearing that the parrot took off, upwards at first into the clear blue sky, then banking and heading back towards the cave.

"Baron Frankenstein!" the Count called out across the clearing.

"Yes, Count Alucard?" replied the Baron, pausing with the monster towering at his side and looking back at where the vegetarian vampire was standing.

"Forgive my impertinence in asking, but you wouldn't happen to have any tomato juice on board your boat, by any happy circumstance?"

"Tomato juice?" the Baron cupped a hand to an ear and called it out again. "Did you say tomato juice?"

"Yes! I did indeed! It happens to be my favourite tipple, but not so much as a single drop of that delicious beverage has passed my lips since I set out from Tolokovin. I just wondered whether . . . ?"

"My dear chap, we have canned tomato juice on board in abundance!" the Baron bellowed back across the clearing. "I'm rather partial to tomato juice myself. How do you take yours? With a generous splash of Worcestershire sauce and with ice-cubes tinkling merrily in the glass?"

Count Alucard nodded blissfully. Baron Frankenstein had described exactly how the Count liked his tomato juice served best.

"I shall see to it that there is a sufficiency of that nectar inside the fridge to attend upon your arrival," the Baron shouted, his right eye twinkling behind his gold-rimmed monocle. Then, with a final wave, he turned again and strode off, his black cloak billowing behind him and the monster ambling at his side.

"A man after my own heart – and the monster is an amiable fellow too." Count Alucard told himself, adding: "Which just goes to prove that you shouldn't judge anyone by their appearance." Then, as he allowed the tip of his tongue to slide out between his lips and run, in turn, over the needle-sharp tips of his two pointy teeth, he allowed himself a little smile. "Just think of it," he murmured aloud, his mouth watering at the thought of the promised treat. "Tomato juice, tonight!"

"Mon – ster," Peppina squawked, pronouncing the name in the same slow, careful way that the monster had done and as she watched the creature and his master move off into the trees and out of sight.

Skopka, who had gone back to sleep, uttered not so much as a sound. The young wolf was dreaming about his homeland and also about his many friends and relatives in the wolf-pack which patrolled the widespread Forest of Tolokovin.

"Splash-splishhh. Splash-splishhh. Splash-splishhh."

As the oars rose and fell regularly, in and out of the clear calm waters, Count Alucard sneaked a curious glance at the man who was rowing his companions and himself towards Baron Frankenstein's boat, which was anchored across the bay and silhouetted against the setting sun.

Igor, the oarsman, was a short, squat, elderly man with an untidy shock of greying hair. He was wearing a peasant's simple hand-stitched smock over and outside his trousers – a style of dress which reminded the Count of the manner in which the countryfolk clothed themselves back home in faraway Tolokovin.

"Extraordinarily pleasant weather, don't you think, Igor, for the time of year?" Count Alucard said, smiling politely at the Baron's manservant as he applied himself to the oars.

Igor did not reply. The old man had not uttered a single word from the moment he had met the three castaways, some several minutes earlier on the beach and he did not show any signs of wanting to break his silence now.

"This morning seemed distinctly on the chilly side," the Count continued, again attempting to draw the old chap into conversation. "Almost cold enough for snow, wouldn't you say? And yet there is a warmth in the air this evening that might also seem to suggest that an Indian summer is just around the corner."

Again the oarsman did not speak, his head bent over his task, although Count Alucard did wonder, just for a moment or two, if he had heard the old man grunt at him in reply? Then after turning that possibility over in his head, the vegetarian vampire decided that if Igor *had* grunted, then it must have been occasioned by his labours at the oars and not by way of conversation. The Count, resigning himself to the fact that Igor was the kind of man who prefers silence to idle chitter-chatter, said not another word himself.

Again, there was nothing to be heard, save for the regular sound of the boatman's oars entering and leaving the water:

"*Splash-splishhh. Splash-splishhh. Splash-splishhh.*"

Then, as the small boat drew closer to the larger one, it was the Count's companions that broke the silence.

"*Olé!*" squawked Peppina. Sensing that the moment was not far off, when she would be meeting up with her new friend, the monster, the parrot was ducking her head, repeatedly and in quick succession, while hopping excitedly, first on one foot and then the other.

"*Ah-wher-wher-wher-wher!*" whimpered Skopka, his front legs up on the prow of the boat, as he licked at his chops and began to slaver as he caught the scent of cooking on the evening air.

"Welcome, Count Alucard and friends!" the Baron called down, peering over the side of his motor-yacht.

"Fetch them aboard, Igor," he added, as his manservant shipped oars and secured the rowing-boat to the short flight of steps which led up to the yacht's main deck.

"Pep – pina!" called the monster, looming up at the Baron's side.

"Caramba!" screeched the parrot in reply and, eager to be the first on board, she launched herself upwards, from off Count Alucard's shoulder and fluttered towards the deck.

"Car – ram – ba!" echoed the monster, in delight, as Peppina landed, softly and safely on top of his head and right in the middle of his thick mass of hair.

12

"A remarkable story – a *quite* remarkable story!" Baron Frankenstein said after he had listened to everything the Count had to tell him. Then, noticing that his visitor's glass was empty, added, as he rose to his feet: "More tomato juice, Count Alucard?"

"Thank you, Baron Frankenstein," replied the Count, handing the glass to his host. "With two cubes of ice and just a dash of Worcestershire sauce, if you would be so kind."

Careful, as always, of his table manners as he watched the Baron pour out the mouth-watering liquid, Count Alucard tried hard to prevent his tongue from popping out and fluttering over his two pointy teeth – but it was an impossible task. Even worse, to his horror, he heard himself making loud sucking noises in anticipation of the treat to come. Count Alucard cast a quick anxious glance around the dark wood cabin. To his relief he saw that no-one seemed to have noticed his slight breach of etiquette.

The monster, sitting on his right-hand side, was cracking nuts between forefinger and thumb and then feeding them to Peppina who was showing off by strutting up and down the table. Igor, wearing a care-worn frown, was gazing off into the middle distance,

169

lost in his own thoughts. Skopka, meanwhile, was stretched out in front of the pot-bellied wood-burning stove, sleeping off a satisfying dinner.

"There – enjoy!" said Baron Frankenstein, placing the replenished glass in front of the Count then, returning to his seat at the head of the table, he went over, inside his head, all that Count Alucard had told him over dinner.

Beginning with the kidnapping of Skopka, the vegetarian vampire had recounted all of his adventures right up until the chilling moment when he had first set eyes upon the enormous boot-print in the sand. More than that, he had also told Baron Frankenstein his family history, explaining how, when he was home in Castle Alucard, he was despised and taunted by the simple folk of Tolokovin who blamed him for the misdeeds of his blood-drinking vampirical ancestors, despite the face that he was a total vegetarian who would not so much as consider harming the very smallest of God's creatures.

"What is most strange about your story, Count Alucard," mused the Baron, "is that it reminds me so closely of my own."

"How do you mean?" replied the Count. "You're not a vegetarian?"

"No, indeed," replied the Baron, glancing down at the empty plate in front of him and which had recently contained an enormous fillet steak, grilled medium-rare, and a smaller helping of mixed vegetables.

"Nor can you turn yourself into a fruit-eating bat during the hours of darkness."

"That neither," confessed the Baron with a little sigh that seemed to suggest that he did wish that he

possessed that amazing skill. The point that I am trying to make is that, like yourself, I have to suffer for
the mistakes made by my forebears."

"*You* do?" asked the Count.

"Indeed I do. Why else, do you imagine, are Igor,
the monster and myself forced to roam the world on
board this yacht?"

"To be absolutely honest," said Count Alucard, "I
hadn't even thought about it . . ." He glanced admir-
ingly around the stately dining-cabin's dark wood
walls, panelled with a faded red brocade which, he
noticed, was embroidered with a baronial crest sur-
mounted by a crown – a sign of a family history as
noble as his own. "I suppose," he nodded, "I imag-
ined that you sailed the seas simply because you
enjoyed the life."

"Aaah!" The Baron sighed again. "If only that were
true."

"AaaaHHH!" went the monster, sighing a sigh that
was both louder and sadder than the one that had just
gone before.

"Aaaahhh!" squawked Peppina, mimicking the
monster perfectly.

Catching the mood of the moment, Igor's head
sank further on to his chest and his shoulders drooped
despondently. Skopka, still sleeping off his recent
meal, stretched his back legs and snorted softly.

"My dear Count," the Baron continued "I also told
you that, like yourself, I am a victim of the wrongdoing
of an ancestor – it was my father's father's father who,
with his own hands, created the monster."

"Your great-grandfather made him?" gasped the
Count. "How can that be? He doesn't look that old?"

"He is a monster – he is ageless," said the Baron, softly, looking out across the sea. "After my great-grandfather died, my grandfather looked after the monster then, when Grandad left us, the monster's safe-keeping passed to my father. I am the last of the Frankensteins and so it is my duty to take care of him – not that it has proved an irksome task. The monster is an agreeable creature, as you have seen for yourself – if only I could get the world to judge him not by his appearance, but by his behaviour."

"Forgive me," said the Count. "I hadn't realised your plight."

"I am called Frankenstein. I am the Baron Frankenstein. It is a name which is, if you will forgive me for saying so, as infamous as the one by which your ancestors were known: 'Dracula'."

"It might help if you began by changing your name, as I have done," suggested Count Alucard.

"It would not do the slightest good," replied the Baron, shaking his head slowly but firmly. He put out a hand and patted the monster gently on the knee. "Wherever I go, my good friend here goes with me. He is called 'Frankenstein's monster' and he is recognised in every country in all the world as soon as he steps out in public. The poor fellow is as gentle as any new-born lamb, but do you imagine that there is any man upon this earth that would wait around while I explained my companion's kind nature?"

"I suppose not," Count Alucard was forced to reply, remembering his own problems with the general public.

"I tell you, if Igor, the monster and myself were to so much as set foot inside a fast food restaurant, the place would be empty of both customers and staff before I had the opportunity to voice the words: 'Three double cheeseburgers, if you would be so kind, accompanied by French fries.'"

"Aaahhh!" sighed the monster, lowering his sad round eyes.

"Aaahhh!" squawked Peppina, sympathetically.

"Aaahhh!" went Igor. It was the first sound that the Count had heard the manservant make since he had first set eyes on him. But it was a gentle snore and not a sigh that had slipped from out of Igor's mouth, for he had fallen fast asleep at the table.

"Saint Unfortunato preserve us, is that the time!" gasped Count Alucard, glancing across at the grandfather clock which was ticking softly and steadily in the corner of the dining-cabin. "It's high time that we were on our way. I wouldn't wish to outstay our welcome."

"You may spend the night on board, if you so desire," offered the Baron, breathing on his monocle and then polishing it briskly on his handkerchief. "There is a guest cabin at your disposal."

"No, thank you kindly." It was Count Alucard's turn to shake his head. "Owing to my upbringing, I find it nigh impossible to get a good night's sleep unless I'm recumbant in my coffin. I would imagine that your guest cabin does not stretch to such a luxury?"

"Why, no," murmured the Baron, fixing his monocle back in his eye and blinking through it in surprise.

"In which circumstance, I will thank you again for your kind hospitality and bid you a civil 'goodnight'."

173

The Count rose on his gangly legs. "The coffin which I have made for myself on the island is a simple, rustic affair – it is not one in which I would care to spend eternity – but it has served its purpose."

"I'll row you across to the shore myself," said Baron Frankenstein, glancing over at the sleeping figure of Igor.

Peppina, too, had nodded off. She was couched comfortably in one of the monster's huge hands which he was holding cupped carefully against his enormous chest. Skopka meanwhile, having opened a wary eye when the Count had risen, now sprang up on to his feet and padded across towards the door.

"It would seem a pity to disturb Peppina," whispered Baron Frankenstein as he too crossed towards the cabin door. "Why not let her sleep here tonight? I'll see that she comes back safely in the morning."

Count Alucard nodded his agreement. "Goodnight, monster," he whispered across the cabin as he tiptoed towards the door.

Fearful of waking Peppina, the monster did not utter a sound, but his lips moved, silently and carefully, as he mouthed his "Good – night" at the Count.

"Splash-splish. Splash-splish. Splash-splish."

With Count Alucard and Skopka sitting in the prow of the small boat and Baron Frankenstein facing them pulling at the oars, the craft moved easily through the smooth waters of the moonlit bay, towards the shore.

As the deck-lights on the Baron's boat grew smaller in the distance, Count Alucard turned his head and peered towards the approaching shoreline where, by the light of the moon, he could just make out the ripples where the sea was lapping along the sand.

"I imagine," began the Baron, breaking the silence, "that it is your wish to be taken off the island?"

"By Saint Unfortunato's holy toenails!" cried the Count. "I had been so pleased at making new friends today that the very thought of being rescued had completely slipped my mind . . . but in answer to that question, Baron 'Yes! Oh, yes! Yes, please! I know that I speak for both of my companions when I say that we would be delighted to come with you. 'Overjoyed' might be a better word. Always provided, of course, that we wouldn't be putting you to too much trouble?"

"No trouble at all, dear Count. How long will you need to pack your things? Can you be ready to sail tomorrow morning?"

"Tomorrow morning would be fine," the Count said quickly. "There is very little to pack." He paused, glanced down shamefacedly at his ill-fitting home-made, sailcloth suit, then added: "I own very little apart from the clothes that I am wearing – and, while we're on that subject, I hope that I am forgiven for my shabby appearance at your dining-table this evening?"

"My dear fellow, don't even mention it. You are a shipwrecked mariner. How else should you be dressed? There is nothing to forgive."

At which point, the conversation ended abruptly as the rowing-boat's bottom grated on the gravelly beach, signalling that they had arrived at their destination. Baron Frankenstein shipped his oars and Count Alucard scrambled to his feet.

"Before you go," began the Baron, "I wonder if you might grant me one small favour?"

"You are my salvation," Count Alucard replied. "My dear Baron, I owe you everything. I would grant you anything that is within my power. Although, in my present sorry circumstances, there is very little that I can offer?"

"Despite the fact that I have travelled all around the world, I have never before encountered a vampire – either of the vegetarian or the blood-drinking variety – and consequently, I have never seen anyone change themselves from human being into bat. Do you think that you might perform that metamorphosis now? Here, in front of my very eyes? I assure you, Count, that it would afford me the greatest pleasure to see you do it."

A slight breeze had suddenly sprung up. Beyond the beach, the tree-tops were stirring gently against the star-spangled background of the moonlit sky.

"The pleasure is entirely mine," Count Alucard said, giving a little formal bow, then adding: "Until we meet again tomorrow."

The vegetarian vampire stepped up lightly on to the wooden seat which he had occupied a moment before. Skopka, sensing what was about to happen, pricked up his ears. The Count reached down, took hold of the hem of his sailcloth cloak with both hands and spread it out on either side of his slim body. Skopka sat up on his haunches and panted eagerly. Although he had seen the Count change into a bat a score of times and more, the young wolf never tired of watching the wonderful transformation. Count Alucard closed his eyes, took the deepest of deep breaths, and then rose up on tiptoe.

The Baron, still sitting on the oarsman's seat, let out a small gasp of wonder as Count Alucard's rough-shod feet rose several centimetres in the air and hovered there for a full five seconds. Then, in a trice, the Count's body seemed to shrivel up and, in place of the Transylvanian nobleman's lank frame, the small black, sharp-eyed, snub-nosed furry creature with pointed ears fluttered on membraneous wings and only a metre or so away from Baron Frankenstein's face.

"Well I never!" murmured the Baron, and: "Wonders will never cease!"

Suddenly, without warning, the bat zapped upwards. Skopka leaped on to all four legs and then jumped over the prow of the boat and on to the sand. The bat banked, dived and took up a position just above the young wolf's head. The pair set off, across the beach, with Skopka taking enormous bounds and the fruit-bat skimming easily overhead. A moment later, both bat and wolf had disappeared into the dark of the trees.

"Wonderful! Quite wonderful!" The Baron murmured softly to himself.

Rising to his feet, the Baron clambered over the side of the boat and on to the hard, wet sand. He gave the prow a hefty shove and the rowing-boat made grating noises as it shifted back into the sea. Scrambling back into the boat, the Baron slid both oars back into the water. Moments later, he was pulling the small cart across the bay and back the way that he had come.

"*Splash-splishhh.* "*Splash-splishhh.* "*Splash-splishhh.* "

The regular sound of the oars dipping in and out of the water provided an accompaniment to the Baron who was singing as he rowed. It was a mournful Versarian folk-song which his father had taught him, long years ago, and concerned dark, lightning-struck Versarian nights, deserted churchyards, open graves and mysterious goings-on:

"Droshka voy, droshka stroy,
Stranka shushkin, slunka skree,
Grashka stroy, grashka voy,
Smanka drushka, slank a shmee."

"*Splash-splishhh. Splash-splishhh. Splash-splishhh,*" went the oars.

"What a perfectly blissful morning." Count Alucard breathed a contented sigh as he raised a hand to shade his eyes from the early sunlight and gazed down and all around on his every side.

"Blissful! Blissful!" Peppina echoed, squawking her

agreement. The parrot had arrived back on the island about half an hour previously. Peppina had enjoyed a good night's rest, on the Baron's yacht, perched on the sleeping monster's chest, lulled by the creature's snoring and going up and down . . . up and down . . . as he breathed in and out.

"Ah-whooo-WHOOO-OOOOH!" went Skopka, throwing back his head and letting out a joyful howl.

It was the last morning that the three companions would spend as castaways and they had made their way to the top of the hill in order to take a last look around. The sun was almost fully risen over the far horizon and, despite the early hour, they were bathed by its warmth. The sky was blue and without a single fleck of cloud. The sea had never looked so smooth.

Only a couple of days before, Count Alucard reminded himself, he had been dreading the onset of winter but now, on the very day that they were leaving the island, the sudden unexpected change of climate was enough to make him want to stay a day or two longer.

"And isn't that just typical of the weather?" the Count asked himself with an indignant shake of his head. "Exactly the same thing happens whenever I take myself off on holiday – the weather is only on its best behaviour on the day when I'm going home."

From where he stood now, on the island's highest vantage point, the vegetarian vampire could see Baron Frankenstein's motor-yacht riding at anchor and motionless in the still water. At any moment, the rowing-boat would be setting out across the sunbeam sparkling bay, to collect the shipwrecked threesome and thence to set out on the journey home. But firstly,

179

there was one thing of great importance that Count Alucard had to complete before they left.

Settling himself on a fallen log, the Count took hold of the large book which he had been carrying under one arm, reached for the pen which was inside a pocket of his sailcloth jacket, and tried to collect his thoughts.

"Olé!" screeched Peppina, seeking the Count's attention.

"Ah-wherrr," whined Skopka, hoping to gain a friendly scratch between his ears.

"Be quiet, the pair of you," Count Alucard commanded, sharply. "There is something that I have to do – and I warn you both, we are none of us going anywhere until it's done."

The South American parrot, who was eager to meet up with the monster again, fell instantly silent. The young Transylvanian wolf, mindful of the delicious meal which he had wolfed down the previous night and keen to sample more of the Baron's seaboard menu, uttered not another sound.

Count Alucard, grateful for the silence, sat quite still for several moments, thinking hard. At last, his thoughts collected, he began to write the final entry in his Desert Island Diary . . .

13

"Will it do?" asked Baron Frankenstein anxiously. "Will it meet your requirements?"

"*Do?*" Count Alucard replied, echoing the Baron's word, and as he continued, he shifted his small sail-cloth-wrapped bundle of possessions from under one arm to the other. "*Do*! It will more than 'do', you dear, kind, generous fellow. It is absolutely, positively and quite unquestionably *ideal.*"

The Baron, who was unused to getting compliments, was momentarily lost for words. He took his monocle from out of his eye, breathed on it hard, first on one side and then the other, polished it briskly on his sleeve, and put it back where it belonged. Finally he found his tongue. "You should really thank Igor and the monster," he said with a modest shrug. "The monster carried it up from out of the main hold, while Igor was entirely responsible for the interior furnishings."

The two men were looking down at a large rectangular antique ship's chest, positioned in the middle of the cabin floor, intended for the Count's use as a coffin. The open chest contained clean, crisp white sheets, and a satin, lace-edged pillow, yellowing with age, and with small, pink embroidered flowers framing some words which were also oh-so-neatly stitched on the material: *A rosy garland for a weary head.*

"My great-grandmother, bless her soul," embroidered that legend long, long years ago. I hope you find the impromptu coffin comfortable."

"I'm sure that I shall rest as soundly in that casket as your respected forebear sleeps in the Frankenstein family tomb," said the Count.

"It has also crossed my mind," the Baron continued, nodding across at the single bunk which also occupied the cabin, "that, as you won't be making use of your regular sleeping accommodation, perhaps Skopka might care to curl up on it?"

"I'm sure that will suit him very well indeed."

"And as Peppina seems to have made such good friends with the monster," the Baron continued, "I've no doubt that they will be more than happy to share a cabin?"

"An excellent suggestion," agreed Count Alucard, sitting down on the edge of the bunk and setting down his small bundle of possessions at his side.

"Stand by to heave short!" The cry, which had filtered down from the deck above, came from a voice which the Count failed to recognise.

"That's Igor giving orders," explained the Count. "Do you know, I think that must be the first time I've heard Igor utter so much as a single word."

"My manservant says very little," agreed the Baron. "He's not the sort of chap that likes to engage in idle prattle, but when there are seagoing matters to be dealt with, Igor makes his presence felt."

Count Alucard could now hear the clump of heavy

boots across the deck and above his head. He guessed that the monster was moving to obey Igor's instructions.

"Check the mainsail!" The voice of the Baron's manservant again drifted down into the cabin below.

"And now, if you'll excuse me, Count, my presence is required up on deck. We'll be raising anchor in a couple of shakes and setting sail. I do hope you have a pleasant voyage."

"I'm sure I shall," Count Alucard said, nodding eagerly. "I'm really looking forward to the trip."

"By the way," Baron Frankenstein paused at the door of Count Alucard's cabin. "You might care to know that Igor has taken the precaution of screwing down your coffin to the cabin floor."

"Oh?"

"Just to be on the safe side, Count – in case we should encounter any stormy weather during the night."

"Oh, dear. I do so hope we don't." The tip of Count Alucard's tongue peeped out between his lips and then edged nervously over his two pointy teeth. "Believe me, Baron Frankenstein, I saw enough foul weather to last a lifetime the last time I put out to sea. To tell you the honest truth, I was so hoping for a smooth journey back to the mainland. I wouldn't care to be shipwrecked all over again."

"Believe me, Count, there is no cause for concern whatsoever regarding another shipwreck," said Baron Frankenstein. "This craft was constructed, every plank of her, to take the wind and weather in her stride. Having said that, I'm afraid I cannot guarantee plain sailing all the way. If there are any sea-going

183

storms about, we may have cause to seek them out."

With which puzzling words, the Baron turned and strode out of the cabin. Before the door had time to close upon the Baron, Skopka padded in.

"Here, Skopka!" said Count Alucard, patting the bunk on which he was sitting. "Aren't you a lucky wolf? This is your bed!"

The young wolf needed no second bidding. Wild animal he might be, but he was not the sort to turn up his wet nose at any creature comforts that might be on offer. With a single bound, the wolf was up on the bunk. He turned round three times, treading down the bedding to suit his shape, then settled down, snugly, tucking his tails between his back legs and laying his head across Count Alucard's lap.

"Our rescue from that desert island, Skopka, has come not a day too soon," the Count chided the young wolf. "You're getting just a touch *too* domesticated – the sooner you are back in the Forest of Tolokovin and running wild with the rest of the wolves, the better it will be." As he stroked the thick tuft of fur beneath Skopka's throat, Count Alucard's thoughts turned to other matters. "I wonder what Baron Frankenstein meant?" he murmured to himself. "Why on earth should it be necessary for us to seek out storms at sea?"

It was a question which Count Alucard pondered over several times that day, but it was not until after darkness fell that he found out the answer.

The Sleep-U-Tite *safe-slumber coffin has been carefully carved by conscientious craftsmen out of magnificent mahogany, lined throughout with soft sweet-scented satin edged with the finest Belgian lace. Fully guaranteed for several centuries against woodworm, dry-rot and graveyard mould, this custom-built casket will enhance any family tomb or communal crypt. Order now and avoid disappointment – if you wait until you are dead, you may have left it too late.*

Sitting up in the comfort of the coffin which Baron Frankenstein had improvised for him, his back supported by the pillow which the Baron's great-grandmother had lovingly embroidered, Count Alucard read the paragraph contained in his well-thumbed copy of *The Coffin-Maker's Journal* over and over again. Finally reaching for his pen, he put a cross at the side of the advertisement.

"The very first thing that I shall do, when I am back on Tolokovin mountain," the Count promised himself, "will be to request that a *Sleep-U-Tite* salesman is despatched to Alucard Castle, as soon as possible, to measure me up for one of those. A second coffin, for special occasions, would suit me down to the ground."

Carefully folding the much read magazine, Count Alucard slipped it down the inside of his sea-chest coffin for safe keeping, then before settling himself down for the night, he cast a last admiring glance around the guest-cabin. In common with the rest of the motor-yacht's smart accomodation, the dark wood cabin, with its rich red walls, ornate polished brass fittings, antique furnishings which smelled of polish, tapestry-curtained portholes, and the framed oil painting of one of the Baron's bewhiskered ancestors gazing gravely down, all seemed to belong to a more elegant age gone by.

"My late grandfather, the eighth Baron

Frankenstein, commissioned the building of this vessel," the Baron had explained to Count Alucard, during a guided tour that he had given him that morning around the yacht. "Then, after Father passed on, rest his soul in peace, and while mankind was making the poor monster's life a misery, I moved most of the family heirlooms and possessions out of Frankenstein Manor and on to this craft. Since which time, the faithful Igor, the monster and myself have spent most of our days cruising the seas, pausing only long enough at the smaller ports, to pick up such provisions as we have needed, or to take exercise ashore on uninhabited islands which, of course, is how we came to chance upon yourself and your companions."

"And, believe me, Baron Frankenstein, we are grateful that you chose to do so," Count Alucard had replied, "for the island we were shipwrecked on was positioned well out of the normal shipping lanes. Had you not come to our rescue, we would most surely have lingered there for many long day."

Proud of his floating home, Baron Frankenstein had shown Count Alucard all over its every richly carpeted nook and cranny, and opening every hatch – with one exception: a metal door which was securely bolted, padlocked, and on which there was a sign which said in big red letters:

IMPORTANT NOTICE
DANGER WARNING
STRICTLY NO ADMITTANCE

"What's in there?" Count Alucard had asked. But the Baron, pretending not to hear the question, had led his guest off along one more gangway, pointing up at yet another oil painting of a long-dead member of the Frankenstein family, in an attempt to draw the Count's attention away from the mysterious locked door.

Count Alucard, snug in his sea-chest coffin, turned his thoughts back to the strange affair of the metal door and also to the Baron's more recent mention of the need to seek out bad weather. But the first day at sea had been a long one, not only for the Count himself, but also for his two companions.

Skopka was sound asleep on the bunk in the same cabin as the Count himself while Peppina, or so the vegetarian vampire assumed, was sleeping soundly in the monster's accommodation. Following the example set by his friends, the Transylvanian vampire reached across, turned down the lamp, closed his red-rimmed eyes and, only moments later, was also fast asleep.

"CraaaAAAAACK – RUUMMMMMBBbbbbbllllle!"

Count Alucard sat bolt upright in his coffin, in the dark, awakened both by the sounds of the distant lightning's crackle and the almost instantaneous echoing thunder, and also, by the uneasy motion of the motor-yacht. By the pale light filtering through the porthole, the Count could see that Skopka had also been disturbed by the sound of the far-off storm and, mindful of their previous shipwreck misadventure, was lying on the now rumpled bunk, with one eye open, whimpering softly.

"There's nothing you need fear, Skopka," the Count assured the young wolf as he scrambled out of his coffin and on to his feet. "This vessel was built to withstand the foulest weather – she isn't going to founder on a reef and sink beneath us, like the previous one." As he spoke, the Count slipped out of the black silk pyjamas (which had been kindly loaned to him by the Baron) and dressed, quickly, in his home-spun suit. "All the same, it's dark and damp out there tonight – you wouldn't wish to go slithering and slid-ing, on all four paws, across the slippery deck. Just to be on the safe side, Skopka, you stay inside while I go out and see what's going on?" With which, Count Alucard pushed open the cabin door and went out on deck.

"CraaaAAAAACK – RUUMMMBBbbblle!"

With all sails furled, the yacht was sailing now on engine power and making steady progress through a rising swell, heading towards where the lightning struck, splitting sea and sky, accompanied by the con-stant rumble of thunder. Holding tight on the metal hand-rail, head bent against the bursts of driving rain on the rising wind, Count Alucard stumbled along the empty deck and into the wheelhouse. The wheelhouse door, caught by a sudden angry gust, slammed shut noisily behind him.

Igor, with both of his hands gripped on the spokes of the huge ship's wheel and concentrating on the task, glanced briefly over his shoulder at Count Alucard's entrance, then turned back instantly and gave all his attention to the job in hand.

"Where's Baron Frankenstein?" Count Alucard demanded, raising his voice against the constant noise. Outside the wheelhouse, the wind was close to gale force while the rain lashed on the glass. "Is he in his cabin? Is he asleep? Does he know we're heading into a storm?"

The small, squat, broad-shouldered manservant, who was no taller than the wheel that he was fighting to control, did not reply to any of these questions. This time he did not afford the Count so much as a brief backward glance.

Not that the vegetarian vampire needed to hear his questions answered. He already knew, in his heart of hearts and without being told, that Baron Frankenstein was fully aware of what was going on. Indeed, there was little doubt in Count Alucard's mind that it had been the Baron himself who had ordered Igor to steer the yacht into the centre of the storm. The Baron had told Count Alucard that it was his intention to take such a course. What's more, Count Alucard had a good idea why that order had been given.

"Peppina!" exclaimed Count Alucard as he spotted

189

the parrot at the wheelhouse window, fluttering up and down excitedly and rapping at the glass with her beak to draw the Count's attention. "Patience, Peppina – I'm coming, I'm coming," the Count mouthed at the parrot through the rain-washed glass.

No sooner had Count Alucard opened the door, pushing hard against the force of the wind, than Peppina took off, along the deck and headed aft, beating her wings with all her strength in an attempt to stay airborne and on course through the drenching rain. Then, as the Count set out to follow, he pulled up in his tracks as a great streak of forked lightning shot out from a black cloud overhead and struck the sea on either side of the yacht, both on the port side and the starboard.

"*CRAAACKLE-RUMBA-CRUMBA-rumble-mumble-rumble!*"

Count Alucard stood stock still as the lightning broke on his either side, as if he had been caught in the blinding glare of a giant's flash-camera. Statue-like, the vegetarian vampire appeared frozen to the spot until the rumbling thunder had faded off into the distance.

Buffeted by the howling wind, soaked to the skin, Count Alucard set off again, following where Peppina led him and struggling to keep his feet on the slippery deck. As the Count groped and stumbled, the lightning flashes hurtled down from out of the black clouds up above, striking the turbulent sea on both sides of the yacht and also fore and aft of it. Although he was careful to keep Peppina in his sight, Count Alucard had guessed already where the parrot was leading him. his guess proved right. Peppina's flight along the

190

storm-tossed boat ended outside the metal door with the red-lettered sign:

IMPORTANT NOTICE
DANGER WARNING
STRICTLY NO ADMITTANCE

There was, however, something different about the door from the way that it had looked when last the Count had seen it. Previously, the door had been securely fastened. Now, it stood unbolted. The padlocks had gone. Without a moment's hesitation, Count Alucard reached out, took hold of the metal ring and then pushed hard. The door opened easily on its well-oiled hinges.

"Welcome, Count Alucard," said Baron Frankenstein.

14

Standing uncertainly in the doorway, Count Alucard was dazzled for some seconds by the several bright lights that glared down from the ceiling. He felt, rather than saw, Peppina settle on his shoulder. Then, as his eyes became accustomed to the glare, the Count realised that he was standing on the threshold of a cabin which was larger than any other on the yacht and seemed to be some sort of cross between a hospital operating theatre and a scientist's laboratory.

"Do step inside," said Baron Frankenstein, as a massive bolt of lightning sheeted out of a pitch-black sky and struck at the sea, closer to the yacht than any that had gone before. "Believe me, it would be safer for all our sakes, my dear Count Alucard, if you would kindly close the door."

Once inside the curious cabin, and with the door shut tight behind him, Count Alucard allowed his eyes to take in the strange surroundings.

One side of the white-walled room was taken up, from floor to ceiling, with a bank of whirring machinery with several glass-fronted instrument panels whose measuring-pointers were flickering agitatedly. The central part of the room, where the Baron was standing, held a long wooden bench on which there stood a

rack containing a row of glass jars and bottles connected together with plastic tubing. The glass containers held different coloured translucent liquids, some green, some red, some yellow – and most of which were bubbling excitedly as though fit to burst.

Opposite these separate banks of scientific equipment, against the far wall of the cabin, was what appeared to be a massive operating-table on which a huge and instantly recognisable figure lay still and silent, secured in place by several stout leather straps.

"Mon – ster!" screeched Peppina and, in her anxiety at what appeared to be the creature's plight, she dug her claws deep into the sailcloth on the vegetarian vampire's shoulder and twitched her wing-tips. "Mon – ster!" the parrot screamed again.

"Hush, Peppina," the Count advised. "Baron Frankenstein does not intend the monster any harm."

"Quite the opposite," said the Baron, smiling as he shook his head then, with a broad sweep of one arm to indicate both the bubbling glass jars and the whirring machinery, he continued: "All of this equipment, which also came from Frankenstein Manor, is intended solely for the purpose of providing the monster with new energy."

"And are you using the equipment that your great-grandfather invented when he created the monster all those long years ago?" Count Alucard asked.

"The very same. Despite the passing of the years, no scientist has managed to improve on my forebear's invention."

"Or, perhaps, has ever wanted to?" Count Alucard ventured to suggest.

"Whether it was right or wrong of my great-grandfather to create the monster is of little consequence any longer. What's done is done, my dear Count Alucard. The monster lives and, as long as I am here to protect him and attend to his wants, I shall continue to do just that—"

"CRAAASSSHHHHH!"

Baron Frankenstein broke off as a tremendous roll of thunder, louder than any that had gone before, shook the motor-yacht from stem to stern.

"Saint Unfortunato save us!" Count Alucard exclaimed as he grabbed hold of a nearby cabinet in order to stay on his feet. "We've been struck by lightning!"

"Precisely so – and exactly as I had intended," said the Baron, striding swiftly across to where the machines were whirring louder than before while the measuring pointers shook and shivered. At the same time, on the central table, the coloured liquids in the glass jars were bubbling with a new-found gusto. "There is a lightning conductor on top of the mast which directs the lightning charge into here," continued Baron Frankenstein over his shoulder, and as he pulled down several large switches and pushed up several others. "The machinery converts the lightning's electricity into energy, which then passes through those bubbling jars, where it is purified, before returning into the machinery."

"KERAASSSHHH-KAAARRRUUMMBBLE!"

Another bolt of lightning had struck home on the outside mast-top conductor and the activity increased on all of the apparatus inside the cabin. Baron Frankenstein, darting between the whirring machinery and the bubbling jars while making minor adjustments to both, was far too busy for conversation for several minutes.

"Finally," the Baron said at last, panting from his exertions and when activities had begun to lessen, "the new energy is transferred into the monster."

Looking across at where the creature lay inert and seemingly unconscious on the huge operating table, Count Alucard realised that there was a fine electric cable leading from the machinery, around the walls of the cabin and attached to the metal bolts on either side of the monster's neck.

"And doesn't it cause him pain?" Count Alucard asked, with some concern, as he noticed that the monster's body had begun to twitch spasmodically.

"None whatsoever, I assure you," replied the Baron. "Naturally, if it were you or I strapped down to that table and receiving the energy from the lightning's charge, it would mean instantaneous death, but because he is a monster, when he awakes he will be rejuvenated and feel all the better for his experience. He quite enjoys it."

"And to think that all of this invention was the product of one man's mind all those long years ago." Count Alucard sighed in amazement, then added: "Your great-grandfather must have been an extraordinarily clever man."

"My father's father's father was a genius," said the Baron proudly. Then, after a pause, he frowned and added: "Although, like many a genius before and since, he was also a trifle crazy."

"Crazy! Crazy!" Peppina piped up, bobbing from one foot to the other as she nibbled with her beak at a loose thread on the Count's sailcloth jacket.

Up until that moment, Peppina had remained huddled with fear against Count Alucard's neck. The parrot's sudden good humour brought the Count's attention to the fact that the yacht was now travelling on an even keel and that the storm noises outside had abated.

"It's finished," announced the Baron, confirming Count Alucard's thoughts. The monster was stirring on the operating table. Baron Frankenstein crossed, unscrewed the nuts which secured the cable to the bolts on the monster's neck and then unfastened the leather straps which held him in place.

"Mon – ster!" crowed Peppina, strutting back and forth excitely on Count Alucard's shoulder.

"Pep – pina!" cried the monster, in delight, raising his huge frame into a sitting position.

"If you'll excuse me, I am needed in the wheel-house," said the Baron, having assured himself that the monster was suffering no ill-effects. "I must advise Igor of our new course," he continued, crossing to the door, and pausing. "With a fair wind at our backs and the promise of fair weather up ahead, we should sight land by noon tomorrow. If all goes to plan, my dear Count Alucard, I shall set the three of you down on the mainland in the afternoon."

"*Three* of us," gasped Count Alucard, as the door closed behind the Baron. In all of the excitement, the Count had quite forgotten that he had left the young wolf alone in the cabin throughout the storm. "Poor Skopka – he'll be scared out of his wits."

Leaving Peppina in the monster's safe, gentle keeping, Count Alucard sped out through the door and off along the deck.

Skopka was lying exactly where Count Alucard had left him: curled up on the bunk's rumpled bedding, his nose resting on his tail. The young wolf opened a cautious eye as the Count entered the cabin, blinked twice, gave a long slow yawn, then blinked again.

"Skopka! We have suffered a raging storm tonight, the thunder has been incredible and the lightning quite horrendous, and yet you appear to have slept through the lot. I do believe that you haven't moved so much as a paw since I went out?"

In answer the young wolf stretched his neck, flicked with hiw left back paw at the troublesome flea which had now taken up a new residence behind his right ear, then closed both of his eyes and fell instantly asleep again.

"The trouble with Skopka is that he's getting too domesticated," Count Alucard told Baron Frankenstein the following morning. "It's not his fault, I know, but he's spent far too much time in my company of late, being fed and cared for, without so much as a sniff of another wolf."

The two men, one smartly dressed in a black suit and a white bow tie, the other wearing simple clothing fashioned from sailcloth, were standing in the wheelhouse and looking out across the sun-dappled sea at where a long thin smudge on the far horizon marked the distant shoreline. Baron Frankenstein was taking a spell at the wheel while Igor and the monster, out on deck, were attending to the sails. Peppina, meanwhile, was perched on the top of the mast, where she was sunning herself and enjoying the view, while the less energetic Skopka had found himself a coil of rope, in the shade, where he was enjoying yet another snooze.

"And does Skopka's laziness cause you concern?" asked the Baron.

"No, not at all." Count Alucard smiled and shook his head. "Once he's back home in Tolokovin Forest, with the rest of the wolves, I'm sure that Skopka will mend his ways. He'll have to – when it's a question of him having to fend for himself."

"I should imagine that the wolf-pack will be glad to see him alive and well?"

"His mother most of all. Valentina's a wise and wary wolf, she'll see to it that Skopka behaves himself. Either that or he'll get a motherly nip or two on his hind-quarters. He's young. He'll learn." Count Alucard paused and frowned. "Actually, it's Peppina's future which concerns me the most."

"Whatever for?" Baron Frankenstein poked his head out of the wheelhouse window and peered up at where the South American parrot was perched. "Peppina seems to be living her life to the full."

"Indeed," Count Alucard agreed. "Since her rescue from the zoo, Peppina's settled down to domesticity delightfully. Unfortunately, the Castle Alucard is hardly the place for an elderly parrot to live out her days – and particularly as I myself am forced to spend a great deal of my life travelling restlessly around the world."

"You don't think that releasing Peppina back into the wild, the same as Skopka, might prove the answer?"

"Peppina's far too old to change her ways – and, besides, Tolokovin Forest is no place for an ageing South American parrot when the winter winds begin to blow."

"Then allow me to proffer a solution to the problem: why not allow Peppina to remain here with me, on board the yacht?"

"She wouldn't be in the way? You're sure you wouldn't mind?"

"Mind? *Mind*! My dear good chap. I should be absolutely delighted to have her join us. Peppina would be someone I could talk to over dinner. Igor is as faithful a manservant as any nobleman might wish for, but he's hardly the sort for animated dinner-table conversations. And, as for the monster, why, his vocabulary's increased enormously in the short time that he's had Peppina for a friend."

"And you are absolutely sure that—"

"Consider the matter closed. Peppina's new home is here with us. She will live out her days aboard this luxury yacht; cruising the sun-kissed seas and visiting new places. What more could any parrot ask for? Now then, let's talk about something else?"

"As a matter of fact, Baron," the Count began nervously, "there was another subject I wanted to raise with you."

"Go on?"

"The thing is . . ." The Count's voice trailed awkwardly away as his eyes roamed enviously over the smart clothing that the Baron was wearing. Next, he glanced down in some embarrassment at the rough-stitched, ill-fitting homemade sailcloth suit that he had on. "The thing is . . ." he began again.

"Yes?" said Baron Frankenstein encouragingly.

"There are still many, many miles I have to travel, once I am back on dry land, and several countries still to cross on foot, before I reach my homeland,

Transylvania."

"I know. You have my sympathy. It will not be an easy task."

"No, but it might prove a slightly less hazardous a journey if I didn't present such a curious and so shabby an appearance."

"My dear, dear fellow, of course you shall have some new clothes in which to travel," the Baron broke in hastily, guessing the words that the Count was stumbling over. "I shall lend you – nay, *give* you – an entire outfit from my own extensive wardrobe. We are, give or take a couple of centimetres, about the same height and build. I have more suits than I would care to count ranged in a row inside the wardrobe in my cabin – you may choose any one of them that takes your fancy, together with whatever else you need."

"You are more than kind," murmured the Count.

"I'm afraid that there is one slight problem," said the Baron, indicating the clothing he was wearing at the moment. "It may have escaped your notice, but it is a habit of mine to always dress in the same fashion. As I said, you are free to choose whatever suit you wish from out of my wardrobe, the only problem being that they are all exactly identical."

"I'm sure that will not present a difficulty," said Count Alucard hiding a smile.

"In that case, how would it be if I were to let you have: a black formal jacket; black trousers; a pair of shiny black shoes; some black silk socks; a frilly fronted white shirt, and a white bow tie to match?"

"Ideal!" breathed the Count.

"And, to complete the ensemble, might I suggest a full black cape with a scarlet lining, fastened at the neck with a polished brass clip and draped, casually, over the shoulders?"

"My dear, good, kind Baron Frankenstein," said Count Alucard overjoyed, "Your good taste is only exceeded by your generosity."

Despite the fact that the lights from the shops, hotels and villas were twinkling invitingly, the group skirted the little coastal town and walked, instead, along the narrow lane on to the higher ground beyond.

Igor led the way, striding purposefully on his short legs and setting a brisk pace over the uneven ground. The monster followed next, swapping one word and then another with Peppina who was perched on his shoulder. The monster's boots came down close on Igor's heels, making the manservant walk all the faster. Skopka padded along in the monster's footsteps, head down and silent, deep in thought – it was as if the young wolf was aware of the many, many miles that lay between him and his Tolokovin forest homelands. Count Alucard and Baron Frankenstein brought up the rear of the party, walking side by side, saying little, and knowing that it was almost time for them to go their separate ways.

Waiting until dusk, they had rowed ashore about half an hour before, leaving the yacht at anchor and safely concealed in a small bay along the coast, about half a kilometre from the town. Despite Count Alucard's protests that he and Skopka were quite capable of finding their own way on land, the Baron had insisted on accompanying them as far as the start of the long winding road, beyond the end of the seaside town, to point them on the start of their journey.

"Oompah-oompah – Oompah-pah-pah!"

The strains of a brass band, playing for the enter-
tainment of the townsfolk who were sitting at the out-
door tables of the several restaurants and cafes below,
drifted up to where Count Alucard and Baron
Frankenstein and their companions were walking in
the half-light before the dark.

"We've often been up here before and sat and listened to that music when we've anchored offshore,"
said the Baron with a happy sigh. "The monster's particularly fond of brass band music."

"Ooompah-oompah!" said the monster slowly.

"Ooompah-pah-pah!" added Peppina from the
monster's shoulder.

"And have you never ventured down into the
town?" Count Alucard asked.

"Never – the monster's very presence would cause
too much of a commotion," replied the Baron sadly.
"I sometimes wish that we might dare to. Sometimes,
when there's a breeze blowing in from the sea, you can
smell the burgers grilling in the fast food restaurant
down there just beyond the church."

"Bur – gers!" said the monster slowly, savouring the
word.

"Burgers! Burgers!" screeched Peppina with a
flurry of her wing-feathers.

"Mmmmmm!" Igor, let out an appreciative murmur which said far more than words.

"Fortune favours the brave, you know," Count
Alucard told the Baron. "Perhaps you *should* take your
courage in your hands, on one of these fine nights, and
pay that restaurant a visit."

"Perhaps I will . . ." said Baron Frankenstein,

adding: "On one of these fine nights."

They had arrived, at last, at where the rock-strewn lane they had been walking along joined forces with the main road that led upwards, out of the town, and disappeared into the deepening brown-and-purple mountain range that stretched, in the fast fading light, as far as the eye could see.

The time had come for Count Alucard and Skopka to take their leave of Baron Frankenstein, the monster, Igor and Peppina.

"Beyond those mountains lies a far-ranging forest," the Baron told the Count. "Beyond the forest lies another mountain range and, somewhere beyond that second range of mountains, lies Transylvania."

"I'll find it," said the vegetarian vampire, trying to sound more sure of himself than he felt inside. "When the stars come out, I'll change into my other self, take wing, and fairly skim along while Skopka lopes beside me – the miles will simply disappear like magic." Looking up at Peppina, who had found a new home on the monster's shoulder, the Count continued: "It's hard to say 'goodbye', Peppina, but I'm afraid I must. I know you'll be well looked after."

The South American parrot cocked her balding her on one side, then cocked it on the other. She lifted both her feet, in turn, and planted them firmly down again. Finally, she spread her wings as wide as they would go, craned her neck, and squawked: *"Adios, amigos!"*

"Goodbye, Igor," said the Count.

"Goodbye – farewell," said the short, squat, scowling manservant who, having found two words that he needed to say had found his tongue at last. He even found two more: "God speed," he added.

"Goodbye, monster."

"Good – bye," said the monster, slowly and carefully and then, taking Count Alucard's slim right hand in both of his own enormous fists, he shook it with a gentleness that belied his size.

Finally, Count Alucard turned to the Baron and, without a word being said, the two men hugged each other for several seconds.

"I don't know when we might meet again," the Count said after they had stepped apart. Because of our separate circumstances, we are both condemned to travel around the world, but if ever you are in need of my help, as I have been grateful for yours, a message placed in the small advertisements section of *The Coffin-Maker's Journal* would be sure to find me."

"I'll remember that," replied Baron Frankenstein then, taking out his monocle with his right hand, with the back of his left hand he brushed away some moisture that had somehow got into his eye.

Without so much as a backward glance, and with Skopka padding softly at his side, Count Alucard set out on his gangly legs along the road home.

15

"Stay, Skopka! Wait!" Count Alucard called out, as the young wolf picked up speed and bounded ahead along the empty, winding road which led into the mountains. "Slow down! We've a long and arduous journey to accomplish – it will take us weeks. There's no sense in tiring ourselves out when we've only just begun the trek."

But instead of returning when Count Alucard called, Skopka stood his ground in the road ahead. He wagged his tail and whimpered fretfully, urging the Count to get a move on. The young wolf sensed, somehow, that he was going home. Animal instinct advised him that Tolokovin and his forest homelands lay ahead. Skopka was eager to be on his way.

Ten minutes, or thereabouts, had passed since the pair had bidden their goodbyes to Baron Frankenstein and his companions. In another ten minutes, or thereabouts, the first star of the evening would twinkle in the steadily darkening sky. When that happened, it would be possible for the Count to perform his transformation from human being into creature of the night.

"Wait until I am able to spread my bat's wings, Skopka," the Count said as he caught up with the

206

wolf. "And then together we'll put some miles behind us."

For the time being though, Count Alucard was pleased to progress at a leisurely pace. He was only grateful that they had the road to themselves. He was a long, long way from home. He did not know a living soul for miles and miles and miles . . . He would not like to have to explain to a suspicious policeman or a superstitious peasant, what a gangling pale-faced man, with pointy teeth and red-rimmed eyes, was doing out and about at night in the company of a wolf.

"Thanks be to Saint Unfortunato, Skopka, that we're the only travellers about this night," Count Alucard murmured as the wolf padded along beside him.

The Count had spoken too soon. The words were scarcely out of his mouth when he heard the clip-clop of hooves and the complaining rumble of wooden wheels approaching from behind. In an attempt to make himself as insignificant as possible – in the hope that the horse-drawn vehicle might pass without even noticing that he was there – Count Alucard dug his hands into his trouser pockets, hunched his shoulders and lowered his face until his chin was buried in his chest.

"Good evening to you, Count Alucard!" shrilled an old woman's voice.

Amazed at hearing his name called out, the Count lifted his head and found himself looking into the wrinkled face of a grey-haired, black-eyed, weather-beaten gypsy woman who was crouched on the driving-seat of a gaily-coloured horse-drawn caravan.

"Good evening to you too, Serafina Krokulengro,"

replied the vegetarian vampire, recognising the old woman instantly. "And what a surprise it is to come across a friendly face so far away from home?"

"I have no home," replied the gypsy woman, reining in her horse. "And it should come as no surprise if you were to come across me in any one of a thousand places in any one of a score of countries."

It was true, Serafina Krokulengro had spent her entire life on the road, travelling all over central Europe and, on occasion, further afield. Sometimes her journeyings took her to Transylvania. Whenever the old woman was in the district of Tolokovin, she never failed to call in at the Castle Alucard, where she could always rely on the kindness of Count Alucard for a kettle's filling of crystal-clear water, or a handful of fresh-pulled vegetables for her cooking-pot.

"Where are you bound for, Serafina?" asked Count Alucard hopefully.

"This way and that."

"Are you travelling through Transylvania?"

"Perhaps."

"Will you be passing through Tolokovin?"

"It's possible." The old woman shrugged her shoulders. "I usually pass by somewhere before I arrive at somewhere else. Climb up here beside me." Serafina Krokulengro patted the padded driving-seat. "You too, Skopka there's room enough for the three of us."

Count Alucard did not need a second bidding, but the wolf was up and sitting down before him. The Count wondered how the gypsy woman came to know the name of his companion, but he did not ask. Serafina Krokulengro was full of surprises and, sometimes, it was best to let her keep her secrets to herself.

"Gee-up, Petra!" The gypsy woman shook the reins, bells jingled on the harness, and the dappled horse set off again. It would be several days, the Count reckoned, before they arrived at Tolokovin but they were going home in style.

Baron Frankenstein cleared his throat, took a long deep breath to calm his nerves, then, mindful of the Count's advice about "taking his courage in his hands", steadied himself to give his order.

After bidding their goodbyes to Count Alucard and Skopka, Baron Frankenstein and his companions had set off along the road that led into the coastal town, in the opposite direction to the one that the Count and Skopka had taken. They had crossed the town's main square unnoticed in the fast fading light, but their arrival in the brightly lit fast food restaurant had caused instant confusion and dismay. Choking on mouthfuls of burger and bun, the customers had gawped with fear at the sight of the monster, with the metal bolts sticking out of his neck and the parrot on his shoulder, filling the doorway with his bulky body. Then, as the cloaked and monocled Baron Frankenstein had led the way down the central aisle of the restaurant, with the squat, shock-headed, scowling Igor bringing up the rear, the diners sitting at the tables had risen nervously to their feet and then tiptoed out as soon as the foursome had moved past. When the Baron and his party arrived at the counter, the restaurant was empty save for themselves and the burger-chef who, standing with his back to them, was unaware of their presence.

It was Herman Ritzik's very first day as a burger-chef. Previously, he had worked as a goatherd on the hills above the town. Although he had only been in the catering business for a matter of hours, he had already decided that grilling burgers was an occupation far preferable to tending goats, and for any number of reasons. For one thing, goats were silly creatures with a tendency to stray. Burgers, on the other hand, stayed exactly where you put them. Also, Herman Ritzik told himself, a sizzling burger both sounded and smelled much nicer than a scruffy, bleating goat. And, while it had to be admitted that it could get rather hot standing over a hot grill, particularly in the busy lunch-hour, it was much better than sitting on a hillside in drenching rain, or crouched shivering with his arms wrapped around himself in a blizzard.

Because of all these separate thoughts that were spinning round inside his head, and also because of the fact that he had some grilling burgers to keep an eye on, Herman Ritzik had not been aware of the kerfuffle that had taken place on the other side of the counter, leaving the restaurant deserted save for himself and the four newcomers who were about to summon his full attention.

"Three double cheeseburgers; three portions of French fries; three fizzy drinks, with ice, and a single portion of Aunt Mamie's home-baked, oven-fresh apple-pie, if you would be so kind?" Reading from off the menu which was on the counter, Baron Frankenstein had spoken in a loud, clear voice.

Before attending to this order, the burger-chef flipped over half-a-dozen half-grilled burgers with a commendable skill which he had acquired during the course of the day. Then, wiping his hands on the tea-towel which he had learned to keep tucked in at his waist, Herman Ritzik turned to face the counter. An icy chill raced up the burger-chef's back and his knees suddenly seemed as if they were made of jelly.

Standing on the other side of the counter was the spookiest foursome that Herman Ritzik had ever clapped eyes on. One member of the group, a sallow-faced, hollow-cheeked fellow with brushed back black hair and a scarlet-lined black cloak thrown over his shoulders, was blinking sternly at the burger-chef through a monocle. A second man, an elderly chap with a shock of grey hair which fell over his forehead and who was so short that his nose barely appeared above the counter, was scowling at the burger-chef in a grumpy fashion. But it was the creature that stood between these two that had caused Herman Ritzik's blood to run cold and his legs appear to lose the ability to support him. Standing over two metres in height and with shoulders, as broad as a billy-goat's back, the gaunt-faced thing that gazed down sombrely at the burger-chef had metal bolts attached to its neck and, oddly, a parrot perched on its shoulder.

"Heaven protect me," the burger-chef murmured as he crossed himself. "My very first day in this job and I've got the Baron Frankenstein, Igor his surly faithful manservant, and the monster they created, ordering cheeseburgers!" Odd though it may seem, Ritzik had recognised, on sight, three out of the four members of the group across his counter.

In happier days gone by, when Herman Ritzik had been a carefree goatherd, in the summer months when the sun had shone and the grass was green, he had often stretched out on a grassy knoll with a book in his hands while his flock of goats had nibbled away contentedly and the gentle tinkle of the bells which they wore around their necks had told him that his charges had not strayed. One of the books that Ritzik had read, more than once, had been the gripping tale of the weird professor, Baron Frankenstein, and the terrifying monster which the mad scientist had created with the aid of Igor, his faithful manservant.

"But that was a hundred years ago and more," the burger-chef told himself. "Surely they can't all three be still alive and terrorising Middle Europe?" Another thing which puzzled the burger-chef was the parrot's presence. There was no parrot in the Frankenstein book, so far as Ritzik could remember. In *Treasure Island* yes, but not in the Frankenstein legend.

While the burger-chef pondered over these problems, Baron Frankenstein was also fretting to himself. Why wasn't the chef attending to his needs, he wondered? Was the man about to press a secret button hidden beneath the counter, which would summon the police? Should he and his companions turn and run while there was still time to do so? Was his brave attempt to treat Igor, the monster, Peppina and himself to a tasty fast-food meal about to end in disaster?

"I'm sorry, sir?" the burger-chef's voice broke in on Baron Frankenstein's thoughts. Herman Ritzik had decided that "safety-first" was the order of the day. He would attend to the spooky foursome's order and hope that they might go away. "Would you mind repeating your order?" added the burger-chef and, as he spoke, he drew his forefinger away from the secret button, beneath the counter which, had he pressed it, would have rung a bell in the local police station and brought constables and detectives scurrying to the scene.

"Three double cheeseburgers; three portions of French fries; three fizzy drinks, with ice, and a single portion of Aunt Mamie's home-baked, oven-fresh apple-pie," said the Baron with an inward sigh of relief, and adding: "And could you serve the apple-pie without any custard? It's for the parrot. Her name's Peppina."

"Pep – pina," affirmed the monster, loudly, slowly and clearly.

"*Caramba!*" shrieked the parrot.

"Coming up," said Herman Ritzik.

Minutes later, with his backside feeling the warmth from the ovens, Herman Ritzik peered nervously across the counter at the spooky customers sitting at a plastic-topped table and tucking into the food that he had cooked for them. The burger-chef was reconsidering his recent career move. The catering world was all very well, he told himself, but for a calm and peaceful life, there was nothing to beat being a goatherd.

"Tomorrow morning," he mused under his breath, "I shall go and ask Farmer Frummel for my old job back. I might even ask him for the hand of his daughter, Eva, in marriage – she's had her eye on me for long enough. Eva's a big girl, and she's not particularly pretty, but she bakes the best shrubel-cake for miles around, and her goat's liver potted paste is the finest I've ever tasted. If I married Eva, Farmer Frummel might even give me the herd as a dowry. I could take on an assistant goatherd and have more time for reading." Herman Ritzik brightened at the prospect. "Yes, it's a goatherd's life for me," he promised himself. "You know exactly where you are with goats – and the only monsters that you come across on those foothills are the ones that are contained within the pages of a book."

"Do you think, my fine fellow, that we might have another double cheeseburger?" Baron Frankenstein's voice broke in on Herman Ritzik's thoughts.

"Coming up, sir," the burger-chef called back. Turning back to the grill, Herman Ritzik gave all of his attention to the very last burger of his short-lived catering career. He would see to it that the burger was grilled to perfection.

The double cheeseburger was for the monster. The Baron, Igor and Peppina had had enough to eat, but the monster had an appetite that matched his size.

"Count Alucard was absolutely right, you know," the Baron told his companions as they waited for the arrival of the extra burger. "Fortune *does* favour the brave. And, now that we've finally managed to summon up sufficient courage to come into one of these fast food establishments, I think that we might safely repeat the process the next time that we drop anchor close to civilisation."

"*Olé!*" squawked Peppina, pecking at the last crumbs of Aunt Mamie's apple-pie crust.

"Pep – pina," said the monster, slowly, and with a long, low chuckle.

Igor scowled his usual scowl and said not a word – which was a sign that, so far as Igor was concerned, all was well with the world.

"This way, Captain!" shouted Albert Hoffmeyer, standing at the mouth of the cave. "They *have* been here – we've found their trail at last!"

Captain Roth, the helicopter pilot, who had been searching in the trees on the slopes below the cave, looked across and upwards at where the navigator was waving his arms excitedly, and then set off in a lumbering run, hampered by his flying-suit, to join Hoffmeyer.

The two airmen, on their employer's instructions, had been searching the many islands, for many weeks, in the vain hope of finding the missing parrot and wolf and, also, to capture their kidnapper. At last, it seemed, they had met with some success.

"Look!" said Hoffmeyer, pointing inside the cave as Captain Roth arrived on the scene. "They've been in there – that's where the wolf slept, on that bed of leaves, and that's where the parrot must have perched." The navigator pointed at some tell-tale bird droppings and then across at Count Alucard's empty rough-hewn coffin. "And there's where the kidnapper himself must have lain his head."

"That's not a bed," sniffed Captain Roth. "It looks more like a kind of homemade coffin. You're right though, Albert, someone *has* been sleeping in it – there's a mattress of leaves across the bottom and you can see the imprint of someone's head."

"Look at this!" said Hoffmeyer, darting into the cave entrance and snatching up the hard-backed journal which the Count had left behind. "He's forgotten to take this with him. It's got his writing in it," he added, flicking through the pages.

"I've seen this book before," said Captain Roth, taking the book out of the navigator's hands. "This belonged on our employer's launch. It was going to be a log-book but the thief has used it as a diary."

"The scoundrel!" snapped Hoffmeyer. "He not only made off with Mr Zeelander's South American parrot *and* his Transylvanian wolf, he also had the colossal cheek to steal our employer's ship's log and then scribble inside it."

"Quiet, Albert," commanded the helicopter pilot. "Sit down and listen to me. I'm going to read this diary out loud to you from the first entry to the last. The contents might well provide us with a clue as to where the villain's gone to now?"

Settling himself on a handy rock, Captain Roth opened Count Alucard's *Desert Island Diary* and, taking his time and turning the pages slowly, he read out every single word that the vegetarian vampire had set down. Albert Hoffmeyer listened in rapt attention and in total silence.

"'*Here endeth this chronicle of our Desert Island days,*'" Captain Roth continued, arriving at the last page of the log-book. "'*I am leaving this journal behind, in the hope that it may prove of benefit to any persons who are similarly shipwrecked and should chance across it. We ourselves are leaving here tomorrow. While we shall not be sorry to bid this island goodbye, our time spent here has been far from unpleasant. There is fruit to eat in plenty and clear water in abundance. Best of all, during our stay, no man's hand has been turned against us. Man, beast and bird, we have dwelled here in harmony and good companionship. I have named this sweet spot 'Vampire Island' – may those that follow after us enjoy times as happy as the those we have enjoyed ourselves. Signed this day in my own hand: Count Alucard.*'* Well then? What do you make of all that, Albert?" asked Captain Roth as he closed the diary.

"Vampire Island?" said Albert Hoffmeyer, blinking through his glasses and scratching nervously at his beard. "That's an odd sort of name to give it?"

"It isn't just the place-name, Albert. There are all the other clues."

"Which ones?" The navigator's brow wrinkled.

"*All* of them." As he went through his list, Captain Roth ticked off the items one by one, on his fingers. "There's that homemade coffin for a start; there's the fact that the wolf came from Transylvania; there's 'Vampire Island', yes – and then there's the signature at the very end: 'Count Alucard'."

"What about it?"

"*Think*, Albert. 'Alucard' is 'Dracula' backwards."

"Saints preserve us!" gasped Hoffmeyer as he crossed himself.

217

"Exactly, Albert," Captain Roth made the sign of the cross himself. "All these weeks, without our knowing it, we've been hot on the trail of a real life blood-drinking Transylvanian vampire count. Just think what could have happened to us if we'd had the misfortune to catch up with him?"

"What are we going to do now that we know the facts?" asked the navigator, darting anxious glances all around.

"Put this back where we found it for a start." The helicopter pilot got to his feet, crossed into the mouth of the cave and returned the *Desert Island Diary* to the spot where it belonged. He stepped out of the cave and back into the daylight. "And the next thing we should do, Albert, is to get off this island as quickly as we can."

The two airmen set off running, hampered by their flying-suits, but as fast as they were able, down the slope, through the trees and towards the beach where the helicopter stood.

"Are you sure you want to give up flying?" asked Albert Hoffmeyer in some surprise.

"It's not a sudden decision," replied Captain Roth, his hands on the helicopter's controls They were flying some several hundred metres above sea level and through a skein of fluffy, low-lying clouds. "Actually, I've been thinking about making a career move for some time." He gave a little shiver, as he added: "Discovering that I've been chasing a vampire has finally forced me to make my mind up."

"But if we give up working for Mr Zeelander, he won't have anyone to fetch his animals – all that he'll

218

have will be row upon row of empty cages."

"That's his problem," said the pilot. "Serve him right."

"But what are you going to do for a living?"

"Something entirely different," enthused the pilot. "I was reading the jobs vacant column in a newspaper the other day. There's a fast food restaurant, in a small town along the coast, that's advertising for a burger-chef: 'Experience not essential, if willing to learn'."

"A *burger-chef*? That's a bit of a come down, isn't it, after a helicopter pilot's life?"

"It's different," admitted Captain Roth. "But it's something I've always rather hankered after: standing at a hot grill, toasting buns and flipping sizzling burgers over on to their backs."

"Well, if you're moving down the coast, Captain, I've half a mind to come with you."

"Why? What for? Do *you* fancy working in a fast food restaurant?"

"I might – and then again I might not." Albert Hoffmeyer peered closely at a chart through his thick glasses for several seconds, scratched at his beard and then added: "As a matter of fact, I've always rather fancied the rural life."

"Doing what exactly?"

"Well – don't laugh – I've always wanted to work with goats."

"*Goats?*" The pilot pulled a face. "Those smelly creatures?"

"To tell you the truth, it's partly the smell that attracts me to the job."

"Oh?"

"Yes." Albert Hoffmeyer paused and nodded.

219

"Partly the smell and partly because of those little bells they wear around their necks."

"Oh?"

"I've got a confession to make, Captain," said the navigator hesitantly. "You may not have noticed, but my eyesight is not as good as it might be."

"I *had* noticed, Albert," said the pilot, drily. "That information comes as no surprise to me."

"I suppose not." The navigator blinked through his thick glasses. "Good eyesight is essential for a navigator. You have to see things in the far distance. A goatherd, on the other hand, can rely on his sense of smell and his sense of hearing when he wants to know where his flock are grazing."

"I think you have a point there, Albert. But what do you know about goat keeping in general?"

"Nothing," admitted the navigator. "I thought, perhaps, if I were to accompany you, down the coast, and then make some enquiries . . . It's goat-herding country around those foothills. I might come across someone who is in need of an assistant goatherd."

"'Experience not essential, if willing to learn'?"

"Exactly."

By now, the helicopter had left the skein of cotton wool-like clouds far behind. There was a clear blue sky above and the sea below was calm and bluey-green while straight ahead there stretched a thin grey-brown smudge which marked the mainland coastline.

"New beginnings, here we come," Captain Roth said, softly, as he began a slow descent and made preparations for his final landing.

Count Alucard, with Skopka at his side, stood waving

220

his goodbyes until the gypsy caravan, with Petra between the shafts, had disappeared around a bend in the forest track.

Serafina Krokulengro had fortunes to tell, and sprigs of 'lucky' bogwort to sell to the superstitious peasants in Tolokovin. When she had finished, the gypsy woman planned to trundle up the mountainside and call in at the Castle Alucard for a kettle's filling of clear water from the courtyard well and a basket of fresh vegetables from the kitchen garden. Count Alucard and Skopka could have accompanied Serafina, had they so wished, but they had already spent almost a fortnight in the old gypsy's company and, now that they had arrived at last in familiar territory, they were anxious to complete their journey.

"Ah-whooo-WHOOOOO-HOOOoooooooh!"

Skopka's ears pricked up instantly at the wolf call which had come from somewhere off in the forest. He stiffened all along his body and the fur bristled down the length of his back.

"Ah-WHOOOO-HOOOO-ooooooooh!"

Thrusting out his neck, Skopka raised his head, flattened his ears, opened wide his jaws and howled, loud and long into the approaching night. Before the howl had died away, it was echoed by a score and more of similar wolf cries from somewhere in the forest. The howls increased, both in number and in volume, as the wolf-pack of Tolokovin picked up the young wolf's scent and flashed through the trees in long, loping strides, to welcome him home.

As always, Boris was the first wolf to bound into view. The wily pack-leader was followed closely by the others; Mikhail and Lubka, running shoulder to shoulder, then Ivan, Karl, Olga, Tanya, Krupkin, Babuskha, Brelca and the rest.

The wolves of Tolokovin, both large and small, leaped and frisked, whined and whimpered, slobbered and slavered and jostled against each other as they strove to make body contact with the young wolf that had been feared lost but was now joyfully returned to their number. There was such a panting and a pushing around Skopka that it took all of Valentina's guile and strength to nip and nudge and growl her way through the mass of bodies and, at last, nuzzle her wet nose against her lost cub's jowls.

The reunion of the female wolf and the only surviving member of her last litter was warm and eager, but over in a matter of licks and sniffs. Skopka, after all, was more than half-grown now and, although he had missed his mother's attentions while he had been away, he needed her to know that during his absence he had matured sufficiently to have earned his place with the adult males. It seemed, in fact, as if the pack had barely gathered together on the forest track when, at a sharp growl from their leader, the wolves turned and disappeared into the trees with Skopka in their midst, leaving Count Alucard alone and unattended in the open.

"Well then!" exclaimed the vampire Count, slightly miffed. "It's nice to feel wanted." For during the reunion between Skopka and the wolf-pack, Count Alucard had been left standing at one side and totally ignored.

Count Alucard's disappointment did not last long. He realised that the wolves were over-excited at the return of their missing pack-member. "Once they have got used to having Skopka back among them, they will turn, bound back through the trees and come and thank me for having fetched him," Count Alucard assured himself. Although, as he also knew, they might well have travelled several miles before that thought occurred to them.

"Well then, rather than have the wolves come looking for me," he murmured with a smile. "I shall go looking for the wolves."

And why not? The sky was dark. The moon was full. Not a cloud in sight. There was the sharp scent of pine-needles in the air. It was that kind of night when it is better to have wings than walk. A grand night for flitting through the forest under a canopy of stars. Count Alucard reached down, took hold of the hem of his cloak in both hands and then spread them out on either side of his body. He took the deepest of deep breaths, lifted his face and closed his eyes.

"Ah-whoooo-oooOOOOH!"

A single wolf-cry far off in the distance advised Count Alucard of his best direction.

Endpiece

The following curious advertisement (partly coded for security reasons) appeared in last month's issue, in the "Personal" column, of that popular magazine, *The Coffin-Maker's Journal*:

TO WHOM IT MAY CONCERN: Baron "F", of Versaria, together with his friends whose names begin with the letters, "I", "P" and "M", are planning an extensive Mediterranean cruise. If Count "A", of Transylvania, would care to join them and enjoy sunny days, blue waters and good companionship, he would be more than welcome. He can confirm his intention, and receive further details by contacting the editor of this journal.

It is not known whether or not Count Alucard chanced to see the message. However, at the present moment the Castle Alucard, which is the Count's ancestral seat and is situated on Tolokovin Mountain, stands empty with its iron-studded thick oak doors securely locked and its ancient leaded windows firmly fastened. The castle's only occupant is not at home.

Scared to Death

and Other Ghostly Stories
by Josephine Poole

AAAAAAHHH!!!

S cared to DEATH? You will be. Prepare for the most spine-chilling, knee-knocking, hair-raising read of your life! This chilling collection of ghostly tales and spooky stories will leave you trembling with fear. See if this gives you the sh-sh-shivers...

I was not dreaming, I swear.

I got out of bed and crossed the room and pulled back the curtains and there, there was a hand, a large white hand, groping against the lower windowpane, like feeling for a way in. I couldn't move, I couldn't breathe, I couldn't stop staring at that large, white, moist hand feeling up the glass.

And as I stared and stared with my heartbeat drumming in my ears, there was a face inching up from the sill, but it wasn't a face. It was all smashed up - it would have fallen apart if it hadn't been held together in the black hood.

SCARED TO DEATH by Josephine Poole
Red Fox *paperback*, ISBN 0 09 928971 7   £3.50

THE DOOM STONE

WARNING!!! This is a grippingly gory, adrenaline-pumping, non-stop-action block-buster of a read...

A deadly predator is stalking Salisbury Plain, leaving a blood-curdling legacy of terror, murder and destruction in its wake. This killing machine must be stopped before it kills again – and again.

In the next split second Richards glimpsed an enormous skull-like face with horrifying, deep, huge eye sockets. The impact ripped his legs from the ladder and hurled his body against the ceiling beams. He was aware of being turned by great clawed hands locking him like pincers, and he was ashamed to find himself screaming. He stared helplessly down into the skull-face, saw it open its mouth. A huge, gnashing spray of twisted, razor-sharp fangs spiralled upwards and began to penetrate his throat. He felt a deep unspeakable pain, saw the burst of his own blood in front of him. In his last conscious moments on earth, he knew he was being devoured alive.

RED FOX *paperback*, £3.50 ISBN 0 09 954271 4
THE BODLEY HEAD *hardback*, £8.99 ISBN 0 37 032281 9

THE MENNYMS
BOOKS
SYLVIA WAUGH

'Brilliant' *Independent*

'Weird, witty and wonderfully original' *Guardian*

'Extraordinary' *Sunday Telegraph*

Sylvia Waugh's extraordinary debut novel about the Mennyms, a family of life-size ragdolls, won the 1994 **Guardian Children's Fiction Award.**

The Mennyms - Granny and Granpa, Vinetta and Joshua and their five children - are far from ordinary. They've kept a secret hidden for forty years, a secret to which nobody has even come close. Until now...

THE MENNYMS   ISBN 0 09 930167 9   £2.99

MENNYMS IN THE WILDERNESS   ISBN 0 09 942421 5   £2.99

MENNYMS UNDER SIEGE   ISBN 0 09 955761 4   £2.99

MENNYMS ALONE   ISBN 0 09 95577 1   £3.50

and coming soon!
MENNYMS ALIVE   ISBN 0 09 955781 9   £3.50

The MENNYMS books by Sylvia Waugh
Out now in paperback from Red Fox

Red Fox Fantastic Stories

THE STEALING OF QUEEN VICTORIA
Shirley Isherwood
Boo and his grandmother live above Mr Timms' antique shop. Neither of them has paid too much attention to the old bust of Queen Victoria which sits in the shop – until a strange man offers them some money to steal it for him!
Compelling reading
Book for Keeps

0 09 940152 5   £2.99

THE INFLATABLE SHOP
Willis Hall
The Hollins family is off on holiday– to crummy Cockleton-on-Sea. Some holiday! So one particularly windy, rainy day, it's Henry Hollins' good luck that he steps into Samuel Swain's Inflatable Shop just as a great inflatable adventure is about to begin!
Highly entertaining
Junior Education

0 09 940162 2   £2.99

TRIV IN PURSUIT
Michael Coleman
Something very fishy is happening at St Ethelred's School. One by one all the teachers are vanishing into thin air leaving very odd notes behind. Triv suspects something dodgy is happening. The search is on to solve the mind-boggling mystery of the missing teachers.

0 09 940083 9   £2.99

AGENT Z GOES WILD
Mark Haddon
When Ben sets off on an outward bound trip with Barney and Jenks, he should have realised there'd be crime-busting, top-secret snooping and toothpaste-sabotaging to be done ...
0 09 940073 1   £2.99

Red Fox Animal Stories

FOWL PEST
(Shortlisted for the Smarties Prize)
James Andrew Hall
Amy Pickett wants to be a chicken! Seriously! Understandably her family aren't too keen on the idea. Even Amy's best friend, Clarice, thinks she's unhinged. Then Madam Marvel comes to town and strange feathery things begin to happen.
A Fantastic tale, full of jokes
Child Education
0 09 940182 7   £2.99

OMELETTE: A CHICKEN IN PERIL
Gareth Owen
As the egg breaks, a young chicken pops his head out of the crack to see, with horror, an enormous frying pan. And so Omelette is born into the world! This is just the beginning of a hazardous life for the wide-eyed chicken who must learn to keep his wits about him.
0 09 940013 8   £2.99

ESCAPE TO THE WILD
Colin Dann
Eric made up his mind. He would go to the pet shop, open the cages and let the little troupe of animals escape to the wild.
Readers will find the book unputdownable
Growing Point
0 09 940063 4   £2.99

SEAL SECRET
Aidan Chambers
William is really fed up on holliday in Wales until Gwyn, the boy from the nearby farm, shows him the seal lying in a cave. Gwyn knows exactly what he is going to do with it; William knows he has to stop him . . .
0 09 991150 0   £2.99

Other great reads from **Red Fox**

Whatever you like to read, Red Fox has got the story for you. Why not choose another book from our range of Animal Stories, Funny Stories or Fantastic Stories? Reading has never been so much fun!

Red Fox Funny Stories

THANKS FOR THE SARDINE
Laura Beaumont

Poor Aggie is sick and tired of hearing her mates jabbering on about how brilliant their Aunties are. Aggie's aunties are useless. In fact they're not just boring – they don't even try! Could a spell at Aunt Augusta's Academy of Advanced Auntiness be the answer?

Chucklesome stuff!
Young Telegraph

GIZZMO LEWIS: FAIRLY SECRET AGENT
Michael Coleman

Gizzmo Lewis, newly qualified secret agent from the planet Sigma-6, is on a mission. He's been sent to check out the defences of a nasty little planet full of ugly creatures – yep, you guessed it, he's on planet Earth! It's all a shock to Gizzmo's system so he decides to sort things out – alien-style!
0 09 926631 8 £2.99

THE HOUSE THAT SAILED AWAY
Pat Hutchins

It has rained all holiday! But just as everyone is getting really fed up of being stuck indoors, the house starts to shudder and rock, and then just floats off down the street to the sea. Hungry cannibals, bloody-thirsty pirates and a cunning kidnapping are just some of the hair-raisers in store.
0 09 993200 8 £2.99

THE RUNTON

WEREWOLF

Ritchie Perry

'I suppose I ought to mention one minor fact about myself -
I'm a werewolf. Yes, that's right, I'm a werewolf.
So is Dad, and my mum is a vampire...'

By day Alan's a normal schoolboy. But at night his 'gronk factor'
kicks in - and suddenly, he's not your average kind of guy...

THE RUNTON WEREWOLF
When a legendary werewolf is spotted running through
Runton, Alan uncovers an amazing family secret - and
suddenly his hair-raising bad dreams begin to make sense...

THE RUNTON WEREWOLF
AND THE BIG MATCH
Alan's just got to grips with being a Gronk (a nice, friendly
werewolf) only to discover that a couple of mad scientists
are hot on his trail. Poor Alan - it looks like it's all over...

THE RUNTON WEREWOLF by Ritchie Perry
Red Fox *paperback*, ISBN 0 09 930327 2   £2.99

THE RUNTON WEREWOLF
AND THE BIG MATCH by Ritchie Perry,
Red Fox *paperback*, ISBN 0 09 968901 4   £3.50

ADVENTURE

The Adventure Series by Willard Price

Read these exciting stories about Hal and Roger Hunt and their search for wild animals. Out now in paperback from Red Fox at £3.50

Amazon Adventure

Hal and Roger find themselves
abandoned and alone in the
Amazon Jungle when a mission
to explore unchartered territory
of the Pastaza River goes off course...
0 09 918221 1

Underwater Adventure

The intrepid Hunts have joined forces
with the Oceanographic Institute to
study sea life, collect specimens and
follow a sunken treasure ship trail...
0 09 918231 9

Arctic Adventure

Olrik the eskimo and his bear,
Nanook, join Hal and Roger on
their trek towards the polar ice cap.
And with Zeb the hunter hot on
their trail the temperature soon turns
from cold to murderously chilling...
0 09 918321 8

Elephant Adventure

Danger levels soar with the
temperature for Hal and Roger as they
embark upon a journey to the equator,
charged with the task of finding an
extremely rare white elephant...
0 09 918331 5

Volcano Adventure

A scientific study of the volcanoes
of the Pacific with world famous
volcanologist, Dr Dan Adams,
erupts into an adventure of a
lifetime for Hal and Roger....
0 09 918241 6

South Sea Adventure

Hal and Roger can't resist the offer
of a trip to the South Seas in search
of a creature known as the
Nightmare of the Pacific...
0 09 918251 3

Safari Adventure

Tsavo national park has become
a death trap. Can Hal and Roger
succeed in their mission of liberating
it from the clutches of a Blackbeard's
deadly gang of poachers?...
0 09 918341 2

African Adventure

On safari in African big-game
country, Hal and Roger coolly tackle
their brief to round up a mysterious
man-eating beast. Meanwhile, a
merciless band of killers follow in
their wake...
0 09 918371 4

It's wild! It's dangerous! And it's out there!

The Shuttered Room

by Christine Purkis

Open up THE SHUTTERED ROOM, a compelling story of love - and hate - by Christine Purkis.

Life is sweet for Alison. A long, hot summer nannying in France is bound to brush up her French, top up her tan and - who knows? - maybe even pep up her love life too! But things aren't so simple, as Alison quickly discovers...

'My God! This is terrible!'

The words sounded loud, strange in this silent room.

At first she felt she wanted to do something. She sprang up and went to the window. Rain drops were sprinkling down, though the real storm was still rumbling over the other side of the valley.

It was here, she found herself thinking. It was here. I know it. It has to be. On this bed. These curtains... a night like this... I can't sleep in here! she thought wildly.

But as she stood in the room, staring at the crumpled quilt, at the impression of her own body where she had just been lying, she knew she had no choice.

RED FOX paperback, £3.50 ISBN 0 09 947231 7
THE BODLEY HEAD hardback, £8.99 0 370 31916 8